Christopher Raymont.

FOLLOW MY BLACK PLUME

FOLLOW MY
BLACK PLUME

BY
GEOFFREY TREASE

Illustrated by
BRIAN WILDSMITH

LONDON
MACMILLAN & CO LTD
1963

MACMILLAN AND COMPANY LIMITED
St. Martin's Press London WC 2
also Bombay Calcutta Madras Melbourne

THE MACMILLAN COMPANY OF CANADA LIMITED
Toronto

PRINTED IN GREAT BRITAIN

AUTHOR'S NOTE

This story closely follows the historical account in the late Dr. G. M. Trevelyan's *Garibaldi and the Defence of the Roman Republic*, to which I am deeply indebted.

CONTENTS

Chapter One

NO ORDINARY BOY?

'MARK, of course, is no ordinary boy.'

Mark squirmed within. He always did when he heard his grandmother discussing him. He bent over his Latin, trying vainly to fix his mind on Cicero's maze-like sentences. Her crisp voice rustled on in the musty gloom of the library.

'No ordinary boy.'

She had a way of repeating herself. She assumed that most other people were stupid. Also, she never doubted that her own opinions were worth repeating.

'Indeed, no, ma'am,' agreed Mr. Bilibin.

He always agreed with Grandmother. It often amused Mark to see this great pink clergyman towering over the tiny clothes-peg figure in white muslin cap and plain black silk, yet completely dominated.

This morning, though, Mark was not amused. Why should they all be scared of Grandmother? She went on: 'I knew from the very first day he came here, a poor motherless mite — I knew that he was no ordinary boy.' An irresistible impulse seized him. In a low sulky voice, intense with feeling, he said:

'I wish I was!'

I

If the bust of Virgil had crashed down from the top of the mahogany bookcase it could not have produced a more startling effect.

They both swung round and stared at him across the book-strewn table. Mr. Bilibin blinked and gobbled soundlessly over his high white stock. Grandmother's pale grey eyes were flinty.

'You said something, my dear?'

He wished he had not. 'It — it was nothing, Grandmother.'

'What did you say?'

Rather late, he remembered to stand up. 'I just said I wished I was. An ordinary boy, I mean.' He swallowed. His hands gripped the edge of the table.

'Stand up straight. Now, what do you mean?'

'Well . . . if I was ordinary I could go to school like other boys.'

'But you are not. Therefore it is much better for you to do lessons with Mr. Bilibin.'

'I am sure we do very well,' said the young clergyman, though he was not sure at all. This did not matter, for, as usually happened, no notice was taken of him.

'I *am* ordinary, Grandmother.' This revolt had been simmering for weeks past. Mark felt that if he did not stand up to her now he never would. 'It's only you say that I'm not——'

'Mark!'

'I beg your pardon, Grandmother. What I mean . . .'

'Well?'

'You think I'm delicate and all that, but it's quite a mistake——'

2

'He questions my judgment!' She turned to Mr. Bilibin with an incredulous laugh.

'Oh, I feel sure, Mrs. Apperley——'

'He knows better, the child knows better. True, I have brought him up since he was five, almost ten years. I have nursed him through serious illnesses. But I am in no position to judge of his constitution. Oh, no! And the fact that I brought up his father and all of them, six children of my own — that gives me no qualification to decide whether a boy is strong or delicate. The impudence of it!'

'Please, Grandmother, I didn't mean to be impudent——'

'Not another word, I will not listen to another word. Upon my soul, this morning has been one vexation after another. I am quite upset.'

She sank on to a chair, her cheeks flushed. Mr. Bilibin's plump fingers waggled in agitated gestures of embarrassment. He turned to Mark.

'You have finished your Latin? That will do for today. You may go.'

'Thank you, sir.'

Relieved, Mark was half-way down the long room when his grandmother called sharply:

'Take your cap. It's a cold wind outside.'

'Yes, Grandmother.'

Tight-lipped and pale, now that the furious blood had ebbed from his face again, Mark came back and picked up the hated headgear. The long silly tassel swished as he went out dangling it. As the door closed he heard her say:

3

'I have to think of the child's future.'

Future. Another word he was tired of hearing.
Grandmother had it all planned. Oxford, of course.
An Apperley must have 'the education of a gentleman'.
That was why the curate came most days to cram him
with Latin and Greek. School, she had long ago decided,
was out of the question. The public schools were too
savage, the local day schools too common. He would
have been bullied, maimed at football, or drowned in
the river — most likely all three in succession. These
fates were unsuitable for an Apperley.

Mark was delicate, she insisted, his chest weak, his
nervous system highly strung. Old Doctor Heywood,
not wishing to lose profitable patients, did not contradict
her. So there were lessons in the library with Mr. Bilibin,
who was glad of the extra guineas to eke out his curate's
pay of forty pounds a year, and weekly French conversation with old Madame Meyer, for whom the carriage was
specially sent in to Malvern. After another two or three
years of this he should be ready for the university.

Grandmother had it all planned, even beyond Oxford.
She would launch him in some gentlemanly profession.
Later, she darkly hinted, she would find him a suitable
wife. She loved getting it all worked out. She had plenty
of other grandchildren but *their* parents were alive. They
kept their distance and her power to interfere was limited.
Only Mark was her exclusive possession, his future her
exclusive concern.

She means to be kind, he thought dismally, but what
a bore it is!

He scowled at the family portraits as he went down the broad staircase. Grandmother's heroes, the eminent and respectable and pompous Apperleys, the men he must learn to admire and imitate. . . .

Sir Charles, who so obviously owed his knighthood to his knack of changing sides at the right moment during the uncertain days of James II. . . .

The Bishop, who had drawn the fat income of a diocese in Ireland for twenty years and visited it only six times during the period. . . .

Great-Uncle George, M.P., whose seat in Parliament had been so unkindly snatched from under him by the wicked Reform Act. . . .

The shipowning Liverpool Apperleys, their wealth based on the carrying of reluctant black passengers from West Africa to the West Indies. . . .

The Jamaica Apperleys, who had prospered by finding useful employment for some of those same passengers when they landed. . . .

'A wonderful family,' Grandmother often said.

The most wonderful thing about them was the way in which they were continually being ruined, yet always contriving to emerge more comfortably affluent than ever. The abolition of the slave trade had threatened the Liverpool cousins with disaster. The later emancipation had been no less terrible for Grandfather and his fellow planters. Mark himself had twice heard his grandmother declare herself 'ruined'. First it had been the appalling new Income Tax at sevenpence in the pound, then the impertinent interference of Parliament, in forbidding women and children to work more than ten hours a day in the Lancashire factories from which she drew so much of her income.

As he turned the last bend in the staircase Mark stopped short. Somewhere below him he could hear one of the maids sobbing. Grandmother must have been on the rampage again. He peered over the banisters and called softly:

'Is that you, Amy? Is something the matter?'

There was no answer but the thud of the green-baize door leading to the servants' quarters.

He shrugged his shoulders. Grandmother chivvied those poor girls round as though she were still running a household of slaves in Spanish Town. It was a shame, but there was nothing he could do. He went out through the front door and sauntered towards the stables. After the gloomy house the spring sunshine was dazzling.

There was gloom of a different sort in the cobbled yard. The bald old coachman, wheezing and cursing under his breath, was pumping water into a bucket, a job normally considered beneath his dignity. Mark greeted him with surprise.

'Hullo, John! Where's Owen?'

John eyed him coldly, then jerked his ivory skull towards the upper storey of the coach-house.

'Packing, Master Mark.'

'*Packing?*' Mark's voice rose almost to a squeal. 'He's not going?'

'I reckon he is.'

'What's happened?'

'You'd best ask him. Or your Grandma.'

Mark ran up the wooden staircase which led to the

living quarters above the stables. This was serious. Owen was one of the few bright spots in his life. Owen knew when to turn a blind eye to his grandmother's regulations. But for Owen, Mark would never have got astride a horse or held the ribbons for himself, never have learnt to swim across the pool in summer or skate on it in winter.

He found the young groom in his dark garret next to the hayloft. He was laying clothes in his box and whistling. He paused to greet Mark. There was bitterness in his voice for all its lilting Welsh quality.

'The news gets round, I see.'

'It's true then? You're going?'

'Indeed, yes. This afternoon.'

'But you *can't*!'

'No such thing as can't. Not with your gran.'

'I'll speak to her——'

'No use, boy.' Already Owen's manner was more independent. He was no longer the groom talking to the young master. 'I wouldn't stay. Not after the things she said to me and Amy.'

'Amy? What's it got to do with Amy?' Mark suddenly remembered the sound of weeping in the hall.

Owen folded his best waistcoat and laid it on top of his clean shirts. 'Amy and me's been courting this last six month.'

'I never knew.'

'You weren't meant to. Nobody was. Your gran don't hold with maids getting wed. So we aimed to say naught till we'd saved a few pound and I'd got myself a better place. Well, we was having a quiet word this morning — no harm in the world — an' your gran steals up on us. You know the quiet way she has?'

'I do,' said Mark with feeling.

'Well, she went up like a barrel o' gunpowder. Called us every name under the sun.'

'And she's sending you away? Just for that?'

'Just for that!' The young man chuckled grimly. 'I reckon she'd send *you* away if she caught you kissing a girl. Not but what it mightn't be a blessing in disguise.' He straightened up and looked Mark squarely in the face. 'I can talk plain to you now, boy — for the first time. You got to get away from here. This place is no good for a growing lad. All these old women — an' that includes the Reverend Bilibin! They mollycoddle you. If you're not soft now, you soon will be.'

'But I *want* to get away! You know I do.'

'A lad your age ought to be at school with other lads.'

'I've tried to persuade her, over and over again.'

'You'll never persuade that one. But you got to get away some road. You're in jail, boy. You don't get out of jail just by asking the jailer.'

'Owen! That's no way to speak of my grandmother!'

'Isn't it, boy?' The Welshman laughed again. 'Isn't it?'

Mark had no answer.

Chapter Two

'I WROTE A LETTER——'

THERE was a lot in what Owen said.

Mark felt more and more sure of that as he sat in the library, officially writing Latin verses for Mr. Bilibin to correct tomorrow, but actually doodling and meditating grey thoughts on life in general.

The library was a good place for gloom. It was a cool, crypt-like apartment walled with thousands of unread, unreadable volumes in musty, mice-nibbled bindings. Here and there stood the blank-eyed plaster heads of ancient Romans. Mr. Bilibin admired these as much as Grandmother admired the ancestral portraits on the staircase. Mark's enthusiasm for both was strictly equal.

Owen was right. He must get away. But how?

He had often heard of boys running away to sea. Unfortunately, he had no desire to become a sailor. He wanted to go to school. But who ever heard of a boy's running away *to* school? It was always from. Anyhow, what school would take him without awkward questions — not to mention fees? Clearly the school idea was hopeless without Grandmother's co-operation. Was there any possible way of getting her to change her mind?

Not much chance. . . .

She had, in her own opinion, all the arguments on her side. He *had* more than once been seriously ill when he was little. His mother *had* been delicate and had died young. And awful accidents *did* happen: Father had been killed hunting. All these were facts. Grandmother added them up, her way, to mean a cautious cotton-wool existence with never a chance taken.

Only something drastic would shift her from that attitude. Something so drastic that she would be even more anxious to get rid of Mark than to keep him at home. Suddenly he seemed to hear, like an echo in the silent room, the groom's grim chuckle as he said, 'I reckon she'd send *you* away if . . .'

In a flash Mark saw the idea in all its inspired beauty. He grinned, flushed as he began to consider the practical details, and then forced himself to face the challenge.

What did old Bilibin say when they tackled a problem in Euclid? Think it out logically, boy. Step by step.

Given: that if Grandmother saw him kissing any girl, let alone a maid, she would have seventy fits and pack him off somewhere where nothing so scandalous could ever happen again, to Rugby perhaps or Eton.

That much was certain, as Owen had said. But how to go on? Mark scratched his head.

It would have to be one of the maids. He knew no other girls. The thing meant nothing in itself, it could be just a bit of play-acting to give Grandmother the necessary shock. The timing was tricky, of course. He must catch one of the maids alone, just when he knew Grandmother was coming downstairs or into the room.

It would be a bit of a shock for the maid, too, he thought with an embarrassed smile — a bit of a shock for everyone, in fact. He would just have to summon up all his resolution and sort of launch himself at her when she was dusting or something. It was the kind of operation which could all too easily go wrong, in which case he would look a complete idiot.

Wait, now. Another snag. Suppose it came off, suppose this passionate embrace deceived Grandmother as it was meant to do? The maid would be sent away too. She'd lose her place, get a bad reference . . . no joke for her, with poverty and unemployment everywhere. One couldn't play about with innocent people's lives like that.

Was his little game no good then? The game needed two to play. The other person must not suffer — yet Grandmother would see that she did. If only some other girl were available — an unknown girl whom Grandmother wouldn't recognize and couldn't punish if she did! But that was out of the question anyhow, because the comedy must be staged where Grandmother would be sure to see it, inside the house or at least within the grounds.

It's not an unknown girl you need, Mark told himself dejectedly, it's a non-existent one.

He brightened. That was it. A non-existent girl, who could not possibly suffer. She could be created out of paper and ink. A love-letter would be enough, left lying for Grandmother to find, like Malvolio in *Twelfth Night*. If she was taken in, it would serve her right for reading other people's correspondence. It would have to be a

letter from himself, not from the imaginary girl, for
Grandmother would twig at once if he tried to disguise
his handwriting.

With a sly smile he dipped his pen in the ink. Under
his breath he sang:

> *'I wrote a letter to my love,*
> *And on the way I lost it;*
> *One of you has picked it up*
> *And put it in his pocket.'*

But soon he was scratching his head again. He had no
experience in this form of composition. How did you
start? The letter which tricked Malvolio began, *'To the
unknown beloved'*, but that would not sound very likely
from himself.

When in doubt, be simple. That was Bilibin's tip
for writing Latin prose. So, with a flourish, he began:
'Darling'. Better not to choose a definite Christian name.

Inspiration flagged. He added the date: *'2nd March,
1849.'* Doubt seized him. Did you date love-letters?
Wasn't it rather too businesslike? He tore up the paper
and began again. He had to imagine it all, like a story.
There must be a convincing motive for writing the letter.
Ideas began to flow.

*'I was sorry you could not meet me yesterday. It is easier for
me. My movements are closely watched, but I can usually cover
up my tracks somehow. I shall wait again, same time and place,
on Saturday. If you cannot be there, leave a message in our
usual rabbit-hole——'*

After writing the last word he wished he hadn't. It
sounded comic. He began to giggle. But he could not

face starting again. He studied his composition, tongue between teeth. How should he go on? What *did* one say?

To his enormous relief he realised that no more was needed. The letter was better unfinished. When one finished a letter the natural thing was to seal it and take it to the post — or, he corrected himself with another giggle, to the 'usual rabbit-hole'. It was their unfinished letters that people left about.

He would leave it here on the library table with his books. But, as he sat fingering it, a scruple troubled him. He had never quite so deliberately set out to deceive Grandmother. Often her fussiness, her tyrannical ways, had forced him into actions that had not been quite straightforward. He had learnt to be cunning so that he could enjoy some life of his own. He would have hesitated to tell her a downright lie, but he had found many occasions when it did not seem necessary to worry her by telling her the whole truth.

This forged letter, though . . . Was it going too far? Conscience told him to tear it across. Temptation retorted, don't be silly. How honourable was it to read other people's letters? He need not thrust this paper under her nose, he would simply leave it with the rest of his things. If Grandmother came ferreting through his possessions, as she was apt to do, then she deserved all she got.

So, he left it. None the less, his conscience nagged him that evening, he slept poorly, and woke early. In the depths of the house he heard dim noises of grates and coal-scuttles, though it would be a full hour before the hot-water cans were brought upstairs. Slipping on his dressing-gown he crossed the shadowy landing to the library. The maids would not yet have started operations there. Nothing should have been touched since yesterday.

Yes, his lesson-books seemed to be lying just where he had left them. Half-relieved, half-sorry, he shuffled through the loose papers. Then he shuffled through them again, more slowly, holding them up to the dawn-light at the window. There was no mistake. The letter had gone.

Grandmother did not come down to breakfast.

That was not altogether unusual. Still, it did not add to Mark's peace of mind. For once his appetite was unequal to the buttered eggs, the kidney and bacon, arrayed under their silver covers along the sideboard. He wondered, as he struggled to swallow his lonely meal, if it could be true that his nerves were highly strung, whatever that phrase might mean.

Grandmother had still not appeared when, at half past nine, the sombre figure of Mr. Bilibin came stepping decorously across the park. Mark hurried into the library, set out his books, and made a final search for the vanished letter.

What was going to happen?

Would Grandmother erupt without warning, petrifying him beneath the lava of her wrath? Or would nothing happen? Would she make no sign, beyond suspending a cloud of silent displeasure over him — in which case his trick would have achieved nothing but harm? Not for the first time in his life, he began to wonder if he had been as clever as he had meant to be.

Suspense was mercifully short. A puzzled but polite Mr. Bilibin was just inquiring how, overnight, Mark could possibly have forgotten all the Latin he had ever known, when the door opened noiselessly and Grandmother materialized like a black shadow before them. They leapt to attention.

'Good morning, Mrs. Apperley!'

'Good morning, Grandmother!'

Mark's greeting was not answered. Grandmother eyed him with a look sharp enough to fillet a haddock. She then pivoted majestically to face the curate.

'Good morning, Mr. Bilibin. Pray sit down again. I have been thinking about Mark's future.'

They sat down obediently, the curate with a bland attentive smile which, Mark forecast, Grandmother would quickly wipe off his round pink face. Mr. Bilibin was used to these discussions. Grandmother called it 'consulting' him, but it meant only listening, nodding sagely, and remarking at intervals how right she was. All at once Mark felt sorry for him. Poor old Bilibin, the loss of those guineas was going to be a terrible shock to his system.

'Mark is a big boy now. Perhaps,' said Grandmother bleakly, 'I have not realised how fast the years have been slipping by.'

Perhaps not, Mark silently agreed. He swallowed nervously.

'A time comes,' Grandmother announced as though she had believed it all along, 'when a growing boy needs other influences. Something more than he can get from a sheltered country home, however well endowed with advantages.'

'Very true, ma'am,' said Mr. Bilibin eagerly. Then, as the possible meaning of her words percolated, his smile grew strained and his voice faltered. 'Very wise, if — if I may say so.'

It had worked! In Mark's heart pity for Bilibin clashed with triumph. So, after all, he was going away to school. His grandmother was saying:

'There is a limit to what even the most accomplished of tutors can teach a boy — even with the incomparable advantage of a gentleman's library like that of my late husband.' With a grand gesture she indicated the cliff-high cases of leather-bound tomes which walled them in.

'Of course, ma'am.'

Mr. Bilibin made the admission with dignity. Mark almost admired him at that moment. He was taking the blow, as Owen would have said, on the chin.

'It is a wise decision,' he went on. 'Naturally, I shall miss my young pupil——'

Not half as much as the fees, thought Mark. His grandmother broke in.

'Oh, no, Mr. Bilibin, it is I who shall miss Mark. You will not. You are going with him.'

Mark's own gasp of incredulous horror was luckily covered by his tutor's explosion.

'But, Mrs. Apperley — I cannot possibly accompany him when he goes to *school*!'

'Who ever said anything about school?'

'Surely, ma'am, I understood you to mean——'

'My views on that subject should be well known to you by now,' said Grandmother witheringly. 'Nothing — *nothing* would induce me to expose a delicate child to the barbarities of a public school.'

Mark sat appalled. His ingenious scheme lay in ruins. What on earth was in the old lady's mind? With Mr. Bilibin, equally flabbergasted, he listened as she explained.

'I have come to this conclusion for various reasons — which I do not propose to go into.' She let her eyes rest on him balefully. 'It is high time for Mark to have a change of air. Travel, as my dear father used to say, broadens the mind. Mark will travel. So that he may derive the greatest possible benefit — and keep up his formal studies as he goes — you, Mr. Bilibin, will travel with him.'

The curate looked dazed. Mark's mind was reeling. Travel might be all right, not so good as school, but better than staying at home. Travel with old Bilibin wouldn't be much fun though. His hopes revived when Mr. Bilibin said:

'I should like nothing better, ma'am, but I have my duties in the parish. I fear that the Rector——'

'It will do the Rector good to perform a few of those duties himself. I think I can ... persuade ... the Rector. He would be singularly ill-advised to go against my wishes in this matter.' Grandmother's voice was full of quiet menace. 'So would you, Mr. Bilibin.'

There she goes again, thought Mark, arranging everybody else's life to suit herself. He felt no more guilt over tricking her with the letter. He was pretty sure now that she would never question him about it. She was too proud to admit that she had been spying. All right then. Let events take their own course.

Mr. Bilibin was asking timidly: 'Had you anywhere in mind, ma'am? I once made a most enjoyable walking tour of the Lakes——'

'I wish Mark to go further than that. You will take him to the Continent.'

'You — you do not think the Continent has been a little too unsettled this past year?'

Unsettled . . . Mark recalled certain newspaper reports which he had glanced over casually. Revolutions in Paris and Vienna, national risings by Czechs, Hungarians, Italians and others.

'The Continent is always unsettled.' Superbly his grandmother dismissed the idea, as she dismissed all ideas which ran contrary to her own. 'It is the nature of foreigners to be excitable.'

'It is a heavy responsibility, taking a young boy——'

'You are not nervous on your own account, Mr. Bilibin?'

'Oh, no, ma'am! I was merely thinking——'

'Nobody would dare to harm an Englishman. An Englishman is respected all over the world.'

Mark wondered cynically if every bullet could be relied upon to recognize one of Queen Victoria's subjects. But if Grandmother had no doubts, why put them into her mind?

'You will go to Italy,' she announced. 'A southern climate may benefit his weak chest. Also, you will be able to study the antiquities.'

Mr. Bilibin's resistance collapsed. At the thought of antiquities his face glowed like a turned-up lamp.

'Of course, ma'am, that would be most educational. If it could possibly be arranged——'

'It will be arranged. I shall send for the Rector this afternoon. I wish you to leave with the very least delay.'

'Y-yes, ma'am, but——'

'No buts, Mr. Bilibin. My bank will arrange about money. You will now go and make any other necessary inquiries — though much of that can very well wait until you reach London. The railway trains, the cross-Channel packets, and suchlike things.'

'Yes, ma'am——'

'Mark's packing I shall supervise myself. Mark!'

'Grandmother?'

'I shall need you. You will not leave the house without permission.'

'Very well, Grandmother.'

Mark tried to conceal his glee and to put on the air of a frustrated Romeo pining for Juliet.

'I think that is all for the moment, Mr. Bilibin. As my dear father always used to say, an Englishman is safe anywhere. So long as you see that Mark drinks no water on the Continent, you have nothing whatever to fear.'

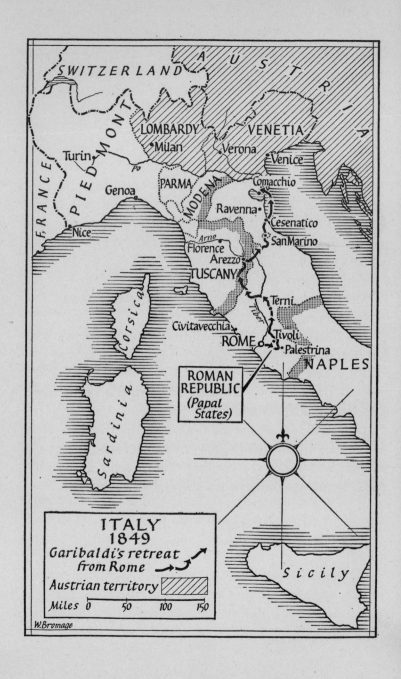

SWITZERLAND

AUSTRIA

LOMBARDY

VENETIA

Turin

PIEDMONT

Milan

Verona

Venice

FRANCE

Po

PARMA

Comacchio

Genoa

MODENA

Ravenna

Nice

Arno

Cesenatico

San Marino

Florence

Arezzo

TUSCANY

Terni

Tiber

Corsica

Civitavecchia

ROME

Tivoli

Palestrina

NAPLES

ROMAN
REPUBLIC
(Papal
States)

Sardinia

ITALY
1849
Garibaldi's retreat
from Rome
Austrian territory

Miles   0   50   100   150

Sicily

W. Bromage

Chapter Three

YOUNG ITALY

G AY voices, a boy's and a girl's, rippled from the darkness for'ard.

Mark listened sourly, slumped over the rail. He felt out of it. After a crowded week of travel he was hungry for company of his own age. But the unseen young people were chattering in Italian.

The night was moonless. The twinkling waterfront of Marseilles had swung away behind the craggy coast. Below, he could see the pale flurry of water boiling from under the arched casing of the paddle. When he peered aloft he could not distinguish the spreading canvas, much less the slender funnel, but only guess that they were there from the blotting out of the stars.

The boy and girl were singing now, one of them plucking a guitar. Mark did not know the song. More than ever he felt bored and sorry for himself.

It was too early to go to his bunk. If he went to the first-class saloon he would run straight into Mr. Bilibin and a gaggle of old ladies. Even loneliness was better.

Would it be like this in Rome? Surely there would be someone to make friends with? There were lots of English people and Americans there. They couldn't *all* be twittery females with parasols and sketch-books. He couldn't face several months alone with Bilibin.

Grandmother had said 'Italy'. But to his tutor Italy meant Rome and Rome meant ruins. He could not wait to reach them. Other suggestions had been brushed aside.

In their London hotel they had studied guide-books, street-plans, and a coloured map of Italy. Thanks to his Roman History lessons, Mark had a fair idea of the country as it had been in Julius Caesar's time, but he was vague about its present divisions, which gave the map such a gay patchwork appearance. He put his finger on a yellow area in the upper right-hand corner, labelled *Lombardy-Venetia.*

'Couldn't we go there, sir? I'd like to see Venice——'

'Venice is impossible just now. The people are in revolt. The Emperor's troops have not yet regained control of the city.'

'Oh, yes, of course, this part belongs to the Austrians, doesn't it?' Mark's finger moved to the neighbouring red patch. 'Piedmont. This seems to go with Sardinia.'

'Yes, but Sardinia is such a poor island that the King lives in Piedmont, at Turin.'

Mark began to remember last year's newspapers. 'Didn't he have a war last year — with the Austrians in Lombardy? Whatever made him think that a little shrimp of a country like his would stand a chance against the Emperor?'

'I really cannot imagine.' Bilibin was not much interested in any campaign fought since the fourth century A.D. 'I believe he was trying to help the people of Lombardy when they rebelled against the Austrians. Of course, they are Italians and so is he. They would naturally look to him — he is really the only Italian ruler anywhere in Italy.'

It sounded odd, but after checking over the whole map Mark saw that it was true.

Lombardy-Venetia was an Austrian province, Tuscany had an Austrian Grand Duke, the little duchies of Parma and Modena were Austrian satellites. All the south of the peninsula, together with Sicily, belonged to King Ferdinand of Naples, who was by origin a Spaniard. All that remained was a broad belt across the middle, the Papal States of Campagna and Umbria, the Romagna and the Marches, with Rome as their capital.

'But,' Mark began to object, 'surely the Pope is Italian?'

He was not just trying to be awkward. If he was going to these places he wanted to know about them.

'Yes, he is,' Bilibin admitted, 'but you can scarcely count him as an Italian ruler at this moment. The people in Rome have just voted for a republic and the Pope has taken refuge with the King of Naples. Goodness knows what the outcome will be. However, all this need not concern us. The city is quiet and orderly, *The Times* is most reassuring on that point. The Forum will be there for us to see, the Colosseum, the Arch of Titus — what more do we want?'

What more indeed, thought Mark with a wry smile? To Bilibin this whole expedition to Italy was just a glorified museum-visit.

They crossed France as fast as modern transport could

get them to Marseilles, using railways wherever they existed rather than the horse-drawn diligences. In Paris the newspapers gave Bilibin another excuse to head straight for Rome without visiting Northern Italy. War had broken out there again. King Charles Albert had marched out from Turin with his little Piedmontese army, in another effort to free Lombardy from the Austrians and help the Venetians still holding out amid their lagoons.

'We must keep away from all that,' said Bilibin. 'The steamer from Marseilles will be best. It goes right along the coast to Civitavecchia — that is the port for Rome. Rome is only thirty or forty miles inland from there.'

And now they were safely aboard the vessel, coasting comfortably along the Riviera as fast as a two-hundred horsepower engine and a mighty expanse of sail could carry them.

The breeze freshened. Mark remembered that, though this was the Mediterranean, it was also still March. He turned up his collar and began to walk round the ship, picking his way by the glimmer of an occasional lantern swaying overhead. As he finished the circuit and drew near the unseen singers, the guitar struck up a stirring march rhythm and despite the tilt of the deck he found himself falling into step with it. The voices too rang out with a vibrant resonant compulsion which was strangely thrilling. Though there were only the two singers, a boy and a girl, they sang with the verve of an army going into battle.

Perhaps, as he walked past them, back to his former place, he would catch a glimpse of them in the lantern-light? Perhaps——

His thoughts were interrupted by fresh voices, angry, guttural, shouting in German. The song stopped like a snapped thread. The Italians retorted furiously. The girl's voice pealed defiance, high above the general hubbub. Then came the hollow rumble of scuffling feet. The girl screamed. Mark hesitated a moment, all too well aware that he had never learnt to box and wrestle like other boys. But it was only for a moment. He made himself go on.

Three figures showed black against the yellow lantern-beam, lurching to and fro as they fought for the guitar. One had his arms wrapped round another. The third snatched the instrument and brandished it above the rail. Its polished wood flashed.

Screeching and spitting like a cat, the girl sprang from the shadows. The youth holding the guitar shot out his free hand and knocked her backwards. Again the guitar was waved mockingly on high, while its desperate owner struggled in the clutch of his opponent. Mark knew that in another second or two it would go over the side, hurtling down into the white mill-race which frothed from the paddle-wheel.

He stepped up close behind the youth holding it, stretched up on tiptoe to twine his arms suddenly round his neck, and then pulled back with a jerk.

'*Ach!*'

With a strangled gasp the stranger fell back on top of him. Mark took a nasty bang from the deck. For a few moments all the stuffing was knocked out of him.

'*Bravo!*'

That was the girl's voice. She added a good deal more in strident, ear-scorching Italian. From the other youth's agonized exclamations she seemed to be tearing out his hair in handfuls.

Mark scrambled to his feet, his head singing. He had forgotten that he was supposed to be delicate. He was fighting mad.

Perhaps luckily for him, his strength was not further tested. Hasty footsteps were fading along the deck. Blinking in the lantern-light Mark saw only the girl and an anxious-looking spectacled young Italian, running his fingers over his guitar as though it were an injured puppy. The girl raised her chin in a defiant gesture and spat after the fugitives, which Mark thought unladylike but impressive, and perhaps permissible to a foreigner.

'*Tedeschi!*' The very word had the right ring of scorn. She turned to Mark and said in a very different tone: '*Grazie, molto grazie!*'

'Oh——' He floundered shyly. 'That's all right——'

'Ah! You are English?'

'Yes——'

'Then — thank you! Pietro, he is English!'

Pietro smiled and put out his hand. He looked several years older than Mark, perhaps eighteen. The girl was small, like the girls he had seen in France, but probably about Mark's age. When she turned her head the lantern glinted on her earrings and the gold crucifix at her neck and the lights in her hair, which was dark chestnut rather than the jet black he had imagined.

'I am Pietro Palma,' said the guitarist. 'This is my sister Teresa.'

'My name's Mark. Mark Apperley.'

'We must thank you for helping us against those scoundrels——'

'Pigs!' said the girl. '*Tedeschi* pigs! You know — Austrians!'

'Why did they set on you?'

'The song! Play it again, Pietro! Let them hear it all over the ship!'

Pietro plucked the strings. Again the marching song rang out bravely against the background of the night-noises, the flap of canvas and the churning of the paddle-wheel. Defiantly his new acquaintances sang the chorus. Then the girl turned to him.

'You have never heard that? It is a new song. *Fratelli d'Italia.*'

'Does that mean "Brothers of Italy"?'

'Bravo! You understand Italian!' She sounded much pleasanter now that her fury had subsided.

'Heavens, no,' said Mark, scared. 'I just guessed — from Latin. Is that why the Austrians didn't like it?'

'Of course!'

'When all Italians act like brothers,' explained Pietro, 'they will throw out the Austrians and make one united Italy. The Austrians know that.'

'They will try anything to stop us.' Teresa's dark eyes flashed. 'They shoot, they put people in prison, in Milan they have flogged women in the public squares. But they will never stop us. Never.'

'Let us sit down again,' said Pietro gently. 'It is not so windy here.'

'You speak jolly good English!'

'But of course,' said the girl. 'We have lived in London ten, eleven years. I remember nothing of Italy. Pietro says he remembers this and that — but I think he makes it up.'

Sitting there on a hatch they poured out their story. Their father had been a lawyer in Verona. He had got into trouble with the Austrian authorities and had fled to England with his family. Life had been hard there, because Papa could not work as a lawyer in a foreign country. He had had to earn his living by teaching Italian and translating books.

'There were many like that in London,' said Pietro.

'There was Mazzini himself!' Something like reverence had crept into Teresa's voice.

For a moment Mark did not recognize the famous name, which he had only seen in the newspaper and did not know how to pronounce.

'Mat-seeny?' he echoed. 'Is that the same as Mazzini?'

They both laughed, then apologized. 'Mat not Maz,' Pietro explained, 'like the Z in Mozart.'

They told him how, years ago, Mazzini had started a revolutionary society called Young Italy to fight for freedom against the various foreign rulers of the country. Like Papa he had fled to England. He had organized the Italian workmen who lived in London, he had even started evening classes for the ragged, barefoot Italian boys who went round with the barrel-organs. Papa had helped Mazzini in his work.

Till Papa died. Now Mamma had married again, an Irishman. Teresa's voice faltered. Pietro said quickly:

'That is good. Mamma has someone to take care of her again. How else could we have come away?'

Pietro had been working for the Great Western Railway Company. He was going to become a railway engineer. His dream was some day to build railways all over Italy — to 'stitch the boot', by linking up all the separate regions and so helping the people to feel that they were one nation.

'Not just Piedmontese or Lombards or Tuscans or Romans or Sicilians — but also, first and foremost, Italians!'

It seemed to Mark rather a far-fetched idea. According to Bilibin, Italy had never been a single united country since the collapse of the Roman Empire fifteen hundred years ago. Since then the peninsula had been continually divided and redivided under innumerable rulers, mostly foreign, and the modern Italian was just a degenerate descendant of the ancients whom Bilibin admired so much.

Pietro did not look particularly degenerate. Still less did his sister. Mark kept his thoughts to himself and listened politely to their enthusiastic explanations.

He would have listened more than politely — in fact with the most acute attention — if he had known how deeply he himself was fated to be involved during the perilous months which lay ahead.

Mazzini, said Pietro, had been back in Italy for some time. He had gone first to the North, when there seemed hope of liberating that part from the Austrians. When that failed, he had gone to Rome, where the people had just proclaimed a democratic republic and there was a fresh chance to work for a free Italy. Pietro and his sister were on their way to join him there — that was what Papa would have done if he had been alive — but now there was a fresh complication.

'You have heard the news, Marco? The war has started in the North again. Ought I still to go on to Rome? Or should I leave the ship at Genoa——'

'If you do, so shall I!' interrupted Teresa.

'You see, Marco? Perhaps now I should volunteer in the Piedmontese Army. They take volunteers from any part of Italy, anyone who wishes to fight the Austrians. Who knows? Perhaps in a few days they will have thrown the enemy over the Alps — where they belong! I might be sitting safe in Rome and read in the newspaper that they'd liberated Verona — our own city — and I should have done nothing! What would Papa wish me to do?'

Mark could hardly be expected to answer this. There was no need. Teresa had decided views.

'We should leave the ship at Genoa! When the North is free, we can go on to Rome.'

'Tessa! I am asking Marco.'

'Marco would land at Genoa. Marco is a fighter!'

'I — I really don't know,' said Mark. 'I mean, I shouldn't have a sister to worry about——'

'Pietro does not need to worry about me!'

'Well . . . ' Mark fumbled for words. He was flattered that Pietro should ask his opinion and flattered that Teresa should consider him a 'fighter', but he was quite out of his depth in these political matters. Piedmont, Lombardy, the Roman Republic, the Austrians, Mazzini — all were still jumbled in his young English mind, and he needed time to sort them out. Only one thing was clear to him, and he could hardly mention that: he would be sorry if Pietro and his sister left the ship as soon as he had got to know them. It might be fun if they stayed on board all the way to Civitavecchia. He might even see them again in Rome.

'I think I should sleep on it,' he said cautiously.

'Sleep on it?' Pietro sounded mystified.

'You know — think about it again in the morning.'

They chatted a little while longer and then said good night. The Palmas went off to the third-class quarters and Mark to the cabin he was to share with Bilibin. He found him already in his night-shirt, peering out of the lower berth like an immense pink, worried baby.

'I hope you have not caught cold up there? I was beginning to think I ought to dress again and go in search of you.'

'I'm sorry, sir.' Mark slipped off his coat and waistcoat in one movement and unknotted his neck-tie. 'I didn't realise how late it was. I got talking.'

'Talking?'

'To—' Mark hesitated, but so briefly that he hoped Bilibin would not notice the pause, 'two young Italians.' Better not mention that only one of them had

been a boy. Bilibin, he knew, had received strict instructions from Grandmother to see that he made friends
only with 'suitable' persons. 'They talked wonderfully
good English,' he added hurriedly.

'I shall be interested to make their acquaintance.'

'I think they're leaving the ship at Genoa, sir. I think
so. I — I'm not absolutely sure.'

But the Palmas did not land at Genoa. When the
steamer stood out into the Gulf again and set course for
Leghorn, he was surprised to come upon them again,
sitting in the same sheltered corner of the deck. This
time the guitar lay silent. Tears were rolling down the
girl's cheeks and even Pietro's eyes were moist behind
his spectacles. He greeted Mark with a sad little smile.

'You have heard the news?'

'I heard a lot of jabber while the ship was tied up. I've no idea what it was all about.'

'It is terrible,' said Teresa in a choking voice.

Pietro explained more quietly. He seemed almost dazed. 'The war is over. In six days! Over — like that. There was a battle at Novara. It was a complete disaster. The King surrendered to the Austrians — they say he has abdicated and gone away——'

'Mazzini was right! Kings are no use — only the people can help the people——'

'Sh, Tessa! That is one opinion. You will involve us in another disturbance.'

'I do not care. I believe in Mazzini.'

'And now we are going to Mazzini,' said her brother soothingly. 'The Republic already exists — in Rome. We shall build the new Italy from there, outwards from the centre.'

It was odd, Mark thought, how differently Bilibin and his new friends looked forward to reaching Rome. To his tutor it was the city of the past, to these young Italians it was the city of the future. Who was right?

No need, he decided, to tell Bilibin that they were still after all in the ship. Bilibin seldom strayed from those regions reserved for first-class passengers, where the English and Americans were to be found, so there was little chance of his running into the Palmas.

Not that Bilibin would have objected to Pietro, who was quite the gentleman and might be forgiven (being a foreigner) such odd habits as playing the guitar in public. But Tessa, with her dark chestnut hair and her sherry-coloured eyes, was a different matter.

Bilibin would not know what to say about Tessa when he wrote his weekly report to Grandmother.

Chapter Four

FOOL'S PARADISE?

'This is a very good address.' Pietro studied the scribbled note which Mark had thrust into his hand, then slipped it carefully into his pocket. 'It is near the Piazza di Spagna.'

'My tutor says it's the district where the English visitors usually stay.'

'Of course! They are rich.' Pietro smiled gently, without envy. 'Yes, it is a nice part of Rome.'

'May I have *your* address?'

They were creeping alongside the marble pier at Civitavecchia. The shouted orders of the officers were already mingled with the shrill clamour of porters, carriage-drivers, and touts of one sort or another mustering on the waterfront. Soon the gangway would go

35

down, the passengers stream ashore. It was time to say good-bye, at least for the present.

Pietro looked uncomfortable. 'I do not know where we shall be living.'

'I thought you were going to your uncle's?'

'Yes. But his home is small, he has many children, our plans are uncertain. When we are settled, perhaps . . .'

'I expect I'll be in Rome for a month or two. I'm going to be horribly bored,' Mark hinted.

'Oh, no!' Pietro smiled again. 'Tessa and I must go back to our luggage. We have no money for porters.' He began to edge away. 'Good-bye, Marco.'

'Not good-bye — *arrivederci*!'

Tessa laughed and called back: 'We have taught you some Italian!'

'You must teach me some more!'

'We shall see!'

She disappeared amid the crowd thickening along the rails. Mark turned away with a vague sense of dissatisfaction. Didn't they *want* to see him again? They had seemed ready enough to be friendly during the last few days. But now, of course, a new life awaited them — relatives they had never seen, a country they could scarcely remember, a patriotic cause to which they were dedicated. It was not surprising, he thought sadly, if they wanted to finish this brief shipboard friendship with the ending of the voyage. Pietro was quite old, after all, almost a man. Tessa was a girl and perhaps——

'Ah, there you are, Mark!' Bilibin appeared at his

elbow, perspiring with relief. 'Come along. They say the first-class passengers can go ashore at once.'

They shared a carriage with some other tourists for the forty dusty miles to Rome. There were no trains in the Papal States. The old government had been firmly against change and had particularly distrusted railways, for fear they brought in agitators from outside. So far there had been no time for the new republic to introduce any such modern developments.

The countryside had a sort of shabby loveliness which contrasted in almost every possible way with the rich landscapes of Worcestershire at home. Instead of the neat black-and-white cottages Mark saw tumbledown hovels; instead of smocked and gaitered labourers he saw ragged living scarecrows; instead of fine red waggons drawn by shire horses he saw rough, unpainted carts creaking along behind a pair of lean white oxen.

Yet, for all the neglect and poverty, there was this loveliness too — the plane-trees with their mottled silver trunks, the pale blue loops and swags of wistaria spilling over fence and balcony, the cypresses standing up so stiff and straight, each like the tail of some gigantic black cat, the billowy purple blossoms of the judas-trees, and faint in the distance, afloat on a froth of evening haze, craggy hills utterly unlike the familiar Malverns and Cotswolds.

After several hours they got their first glimpse of Rome and Bilibin's mounting excitement became more than he could bear. He leant dangerously far out of the carriage window, rather (thought Mark) like a great

sausage bursting out of a sausage-roll. He exclaimed, he explained, he dribbled Latin quotations which neither Mark nor any of the other passengers could understand.

'This very road! Think, my boy — it must be the Via Aurelia. It was here before Julius Caesar was born!'

'Then I guess it's time they built a new one,' said an American lady who had already complained of the bumps.

Her husband, peering through the left-hand window, announced that he could see the dome of St. Peter's rising above the battlements of the Vatican Hill. There was a chorus of excited exclamations, in which Bilibin did not join. Anything constructed within the last fifteen hundred years seemed to him unworthy of notice.

For some little way their road ran parallel with the city wall, then it swung slightly to the left and they saw, at the foot of a dip, the arch of the Porta Cavalleggieri, through which, after brief formalities, the officials waved them on.

'Rome at last, sir!'

'Hardly, my boy. This was never more than an outer suburb. The real Rome lies east of the Tiber.'

In a few moments they were skirting a vast square with curving colonnades. Mark craned his neck with the others to catch a glimpse of St. Peter's, the immense façade and the row of apostolic statues silhouetted against the orange sky. Then the carriage swung away with a clatter and the next landmark loomed before them, a massive drum-shaped bastion.

'Say, I recognize that from the engravings!' cried the American lady. 'Isn't that the Castel Sant' Angelo?'

'That, madam,' Bilibin corrected her, 'is the mausoleum of the Emperor Hadrian.'

'But my picture back home says——'

'It was turned into a fortress by later popes and kings,' Bilibin admitted with deep disapproval. 'Properly, it is the tomb of all the emperors from Hadrian to Caracalla.'

'My!' said the American lady, making the best of it.

Bilibin's spirits rose again as they drove across the bridge. At last he was entering the Rome of Cicero and Virgil. He mumbled more quotations. Nobody listened.

Mark was cheerful too, but for the opposite reason: so far there was not a ruin in sight. The streets were

D

crowded and gay. Carriages spanked up and down, there were café-tables on the pavement, and the shops were beginning to glow with lights. All was life and noise and colour — ladies in fashionable bonnets and top-hatted gentlemen, bearded artists with canvases under their arms, soldiers in strangely varied uniforms, priests in even stranger hats, sandalled friars, and impudent guttersnipes darting in and out of the traffic like minnows.

In a few minutes they reached the Piazza di Spagna. Behind a sparkling fountain a broad stairway curved up between ornamental balustrades, banked with baskets of spring flowers, yellow and pink and white, and sprays of lilac. At the top, ghostly in the gathering twilight, stood a twin-towered church, unlike any church he had ever seen in England.

'My! The Spanish Steps! And I guess the house at the bottom is where that poor young Keats died!'

'Indeed, madam?' said Bilibin, as though it were the best thing that Keats could have done. Had it been Catullus now, or Horace . . . ! But a modern English poet, alive until thirty years ago, was of minor interest.

The lodgings which had been recommended to them stood at the very next turning and Mark found that he could see a corner of the piazza from the balcony of his second-floor bedroom. Bilibin had the adjoining room, and they shared a big living-room on the floor below. Here, as soon as they had washed off the dust of the journey, they found their landlord fussing round the candle-lit supper-table.

'Everything is ready for the *signori*! To commence, the soup. Ver' good soup, what we call *vermicelli*, you will like, yes! And after? The turkey, the veal, the cheese-cakes, the fruit——'

'Excellent,' said Bilibin, tucking in his napkin.

'And to drink? The red wine or the white? For the young *signore* perhaps the white wine of Orvieto?'

'The young *signore* will not drink wine,' said Bilibin firmly. 'Nor will he drink water.'

'Tea then? Often I am serving the English people!'

'We will both take tea — after the meal. Meanwhile, yes — yes, I think I will sample a very small bottle of this wine you recommend.'

'At once, *signore!*'

Half an hour later Bilibin wiped his lips and said: 'I think we shall be very comfortable here for a few weeks.'

'Jolly good grub, sir, anyhow.'

'Excellent.' Bilibin looked for once as if he had not a care in the world, but with a conscientious effort he went on: 'Tomorrow we must unpack our books.'

'Yes, sir.'

'We must draw up a scheme of study. In the mornings and evenings we shall visit sites of classical antiquity.'

'Yes, sir.'

'In the afternoons we can draw these blinds against the heat and proceed with our usual lessons.'

Mark groaned inwardly. 'Could we go out tonight, sir, just for a little while, and explore?'

'You are not overtired, my dear boy? It might certainly do us good to take a turn in the fresh air.' Bilibin mopped his face, which for some reason was several shades pinker than usual.

He reappeared a few minutes later, his top hat tilted at an almost rakish angle. Bilibin (thought Mark) was coming on. As Grandmother's shadow receded into the distance he seemed less and less the timid curate. Being abroad must help. At home the very cut and colour of his clothes suggested a clergyman. Here, where the priests wore long black robes and flat hats with spreading brims, nobody would have guessed his religious calling.

Mark himself had been allowed to exchange his tasselled cap for a bowler, a more suitable headgear for a boy old enough to tour the Continent with his tutor.

The piazza was now livelier than ever. More carriages jingled by, music throbbed from the cafés, the night was fragrant with scent and cigars.

'Rather fun, sir,' Mark said, 'walking along here where nobody knows us from Adam.' If you went out in Malvern there were few surprises. You knew almost everybody. What was worse, they knew you. If you did anything the least bit unusual, it was all over the district in no time, and someone had told Grandmother before you reached home.

'Very pleasant,' agreed Bilibin contentedly. He almost swaggered in his new-found sense of freedom.

Hardly were the words out of his mouth when a rugged Scots voice was heard behind them:

'Well, I'll be hanged! Bilibin!'

They spun round together. An immense, unkempt, sandy young man had risen from one of the café-tables. Blue eyes twinkled mischievously. The craggy features

42

were quarried by an explosive grin. To Mark's mingled
horror and delight the stranger burst into song:

'Where've ye been a' the day, Bilibin, Bilibin?
Where've ye been a' the day, my Bilibin?'

The curate went purple.

'Upon my soul! MacWhirter!'

'Haven't seen you since Oxford! What on earth are
you doing here?' The blue eyes rested on Mark with
amusement. 'Bear-leading, eh?'

'I — I *am* doing a little tutoring. This is my pupil,
Mark Apperley. Mark, this is Mr. MacWhirter. An old
College friend.'

Mark winced as a powerful paw engulfed his hand.
He knew that 'bear-leading' was the accepted term for
taking a pupil abroad, but if anyone resembled a bear it
was the Scotsman rather than himself. As MacWhirter
curved his great arms around them and pressed them
down into the vacant seats at his table, he suggested
nothing so much as an amiable grizzly in blue check
trousers, sprigged waistcoat, and flowing tie.

'This calls for celebration!' He beckoned the waiter
and ordered brandy. 'The laddie had better have an ice,
I suppose?'

'Thank you, sir——'

'Rot-gut stuff, but old Bilibin will have a fit if I offer
you anything else. And these Italian ices are reckoned
something special, if you like that sort of thing.'

Mark found that he most certainly did.

MacWhirter removed a sketch-book from the table to

make room for the glasses. Mark caught a glimpse of some drawings. He was relieved to see that they were not of mouldering ruins but of living faces — a soldier with a fierce moustache, a workman in a knitted cap of Liberty, a market-woman.

'You still amuse yourself with your pencil?' said Bilibin.

'Amuse myself be——!' MacWhirter stopped, swallowed visibly, then growled: 'Out of respect to your sacred calling and this laddie's tender years, I will merely say, "be hanged!" But look for yourself.' Indignantly he leafed through the book. Mark got brief glimpses of sentries at gates and orators at street-corners, of assemblies, processions, portraits. One bore the scribbled caption, *Mazzini*, and he had just time to see how vividly the artist had caught the piercing eyes and massive forehead, the strong straight nose and thick beard, of the man who was such a hero to Pietro and his sister.

'I say, sir, these are jolly good!'

'Mr. MacWhirter was always extremely talented,' Bilibin hastily agreed. 'At Oxford, indeed, his artistic interests got in the way of his studies——'

'I was sent down,' said MacWhirter with a chuckle.

'So I recall. And what have you been doing since?' Bilibin eyed his old friend a little nervously, lest the answer might be too scandalous for Mark's ears.

'Oh, this and that. Journalism, mostly.'

'Journalism? But you could never even spell!'

MacWhirter flung back his head and hooted.

'Och! Printers can spell. Dictionaries can spell. Let 'em get on with it. *This* is my journalism.' He tapped

44

the sketch-book. 'Better than words. I show the public, I don't just describe. They *see* the news — and the personalities. Amuse myself, indeed!' He wagged a bony finger under Bilibin's nose. 'You see before you, my dear fellow, the Special Correspondent of the *Pictorial Chronicle*!' As Bilibin looked more mystified than impressed, he went on in a less dramatic tone: 'I know it doesn't come up to the *Illustrated London News*, but give us a chance, it only started last year.'

'You mean — this paper pays you? Just to be in Rome and draw pictures?'

'Just to draw my little pictures, Bilibin! Ay, just to amuse myself with my pencil, as you call it!'

'My dear MacWhirter — forgive me — I do assure you——'

'That's all right!'

'I know nothing of journalism. I do not understand why a London weekly newspaper should go to the expense of keeping a man here in Rome——'

'Because, my dear fellow, Rome's the place where things are going to happen. And happen fast. It'll be too late when the news actually starts coming through on the electrical thingummy——'

'The electro-magnetic telegraph?' Mark suggested, proud of his up-to-date knowledge.

'Ay, that contraption. News in a twinkling. But not pictures. And it's pictures the modern public want! No good then, telling the artists to pack their bags and start for Italy. Might be all over before they got there.'

Bilibin blinked. His new-found confidence was ebbing away. 'What might be all over? You don't mean that something sensational is likely to happen? Here in Rome?'

'Here in Rome, my dear old other-worldly, up-in-the-clouds, is-Caesar-dead-yet companion of my ill-spent youth! Have you not realised it? Here in Rome we're sitting on a volcano. Any day now the thing may boil over.'

'You alarm me, MacWhirter. I beg of you, explain.'

'If I'm going to explain, we'd better have another brandy each. I'm thinking you may need yours.'

Politics again, thought Mark. But he listened intently, partly because he had been brought up to listen respectfully to grown-ups, however boring their conversation, and partly because, since meeting Pietro and Tessa, he had begun to realise that Italian politics need not be boring at all. They were an exciting drama in which even ordinary young people like his two friends on the voyage might be caught up. It was late, and he was tired after the long day, but he was certainly not going to remind Bilibin about bedtime. It was worth making an effort to concentrate and understand.

'It's all historical,' MacWhirter was explaining. 'I don't know any history. But I gather that Rome and the Papal States have formed a separate territory for donkey's years.'

'Since the fall of the Roman Empire,' said Bilibin.

'I'll not contradict you. Now, you see where that gets us? Or rather the Pope? He's not only the Holy Father, earthly head of the Roman Catholic Church. He's also a ruling sovereign. Like the King o' Naples — or our own Queen Victoria.'

'Two different things at once,' Mark murmured.

46

'Different's the word, laddie. Just as the Queen has to pass a lot o' things over to ministers and secretaries and suchlike, so His Holiness has to rule through his cardinals and so forth. His religious leadership may be fine — no need to go into that. His government o' the Papal States may be fine. But it doesn't follow. You laid your finger on it. They're two utterly different things. You may be the most devout Roman Catholic, the most devoted and obedient follower of the Holy Father in every tiniest point of your religion — but you may still have your own critical opinion of the way the Papal States have been governed.'

'Is there any reason why they *should* be governed any better than other states?' Mark asked.

'You've a quick understanding. Old Bilibin must have more ideas than I thought. As a matter of fact, laddie, up to three years ago, the government here was a sight worse than most. What with police spies, people beaten and jailed and driven into exile — I could tell you a few stories——'

'What happened three years ago, sir?'

'Pio Nono.'

'Pio Nono?'

'The election of the new Pope. Pius the Ninth. Pio Nono in Italian. You'll have to learn some Italian if you stay here, or you won't understand anything and you'll have no fun at all.'

'Mark has to concentrate on his Latin and Greek,' said Bilibin quickly. 'And he is not in Rome for fun. But do get on with your explanation, MacWhirter, and don't keep us in suspense.'

47

'I am getting on! Only a fool expects complicated matters to be explained in a couple of minutes.'

The artist was allowed to go on for some time without any more interruptions.

He described the people's joy at the election of the new Pope, who was known to be a kindly man with liberal sympathies. He had begun by setting free hundreds of political prisoners and letting hundreds of exiles return to their homes. He had started to clean up the corruption and backwardness of the Papal States. He had become a hero to freedom-loving Italians everywhere.

'They altered some of the choruses in the opera-houses,' said MacWhirter. 'They put in fresh words in praise of Pio Nono. But it was too good to last.'

He explained how the new Pope had gone too fast for many of his most powerful followers, but too slow for the democratic parties. Even a Pope could not do exactly as he liked. His hands were tied.

To make matters even more awkward, there was Mazzini's growing movement for one united Italy. Lombardy and Venice had struggled to throw out the Austrians — Venice was still defying the Austrian armies — and Piedmont had done her best to help. The people of Rome and the Papal States wanted to play their part, too, and demanded that their government should join any war of liberation against the Austrian Emperor.

'And that's where it's so deuced awkward,' Mac-Whirter explained. 'I mean, for a man who is not only ruler of the Papal States but also the leader of the Roman

Catholic Church throughout the world. The Emperor is a loyal member of that Church. Pio Nono said, how could he declare war against him? Pio Nono said he must be neutral. But the patriotic Italians said that nobody *could* be neutral, not while Austrians lorded it over so much of Italy.'

'A distressing dilemma,' said Bilibin.

Things had come to a head a few months ago. Pio Nono's prime minister had been assassinated. A new government had been formed, but the Pope had felt unable to agree to its policy. He had left Rome secretly and taken refuge with the King of Naples. The Assembly had voted, by a huge majority, for the Roman Republic which was now in existence — and which many hoped would be the nucleus of a new Italian state when the other parts of the peninsula were free to join up with it. That was why Mazzini, though himself a northerner from Piedmont, had come from England and taken the leading position in the Roman government.

Mark thought of Pietro and Tessa. He saw now why they had chosen this particular moment to leave London and to make not for their native Verona but for Rome, where they had never set foot in their lives before.

'Mind you,' MacWhirter was saying, 'the Holy Father could come back here tomorrow — the people want him back, Rome doesn't feel like Rome without the Pope. But he can only come back as the leader of the Church, not as their political ruler. He can't be both. There it is. Very painful — and not only for him. These people —' MacWhirter waved his hand to indicate the whole crowded café, the unending stream of passers-by

49

along the pavement — 'these people are almost all of them devout Roman Catholics. They're not enjoying this rumpus.'

Again Mark remembered his young friends. There had been a Sunday at sea. Pietro and Tessa had been much keener to attend Mass than he himself had been to hear Bilibin read Morning Prayer to the English tourists in the first-class saloon.

'Will the Pope come back, sir?' he asked.

'How can he — on their terms? Pio Nono sees himself as the heir to all the Popes who have ever been. How can he give up what he regards as his proper rights? Remember, he's got to guard those rights and pass them on to the Popes who come after him.'

'Extraordinarily difficult,' sighed Bilibin. 'But what can he *do*? He has no army to fight these republicans.'

'Not of his own. The Papal troops — such as they are — stayed behind and took the oath to the new government. You see them about the streets as well as the Civic Guard. No, but other people have armies. Pio Nono has issued an appeal to all the Catholic governments of Europe — but above all to Austria, France, Spain and Naples. Who'd like the honour of restoring him to his throne in St. Peter's? The invitation is open.' MacWhirter's voice had suddenly become grim. Bilibin stared anxiously across the table.

'Do you mean to say——'

'I mean,' said MacWhirter quietly, 'that it looks like being a race to see which army gets here first.' His eyes, no longer twinkling, roved coldly over the people chattering at the other tables. 'These folk are living in a fool's paradise. You know how you hunt tigers in India? You tether a goat and watch for the tigers to come prowling out of the jungle. Well, Rome's the goat. Soon we shall have half a dozen tigers converging from various points of the compass. Unfortunately for the goat, there's just nobody here with the right size of gun!'

Chapter Five

RED, WHITE AND GREEN

'D EAR *Grandmother — We have now been in Rome a week and I find it all very instructive.*'

Mark paused to chew his pen. The secret of editing, MacWhirter had assured him, was knowing what to leave out. MacWhirter said a lot of things which were not meant to be taken too seriously, but on this point Mark agreed with him. Letters home called for considerable editorial skill.

'*Every day we visit historical sites. We have studied the Forum, Pantheon, Colosseum, Arch of Titus, and Baths of Caracalla. There is no water in them now (the Baths), but there are fountains everywhere, which is pleasant because we get so hot walking, especially Mr. Bilibin.*'

Would it be safer to miss out MacWhirter? But the letter must not be too short. He went on, carefully:

'*We have met a Scotch gentleman who was at Oxford with Mr. Bilibin. He knows Italian and is very helpful to us.*' Better not say that MacWhirter was an artist. Grandmother distrusted artists. Journalism was not very respectable either. Mark wrote simply: '*He knows about Art, he explains things very clearly, and I have learnt a lot from him.*'

That was true enough. MacWhirter had attached

himself to all their expeditions. Mark found his worldly
wisdom and cynical humour a welcome relief from
Bilibin's learned monologues. In the evenings the three
usually met again at the Café Bon Goût in the piazza
near by or at the more palatial Café Nuovo. MacWhirter
could hold forth fascinatingly on any topic under the
sun, but after that first conversation he seemed unwilling
to discuss the crisis looming over Rome.

Mark tackled him on the subject one morning as they
sat amid the ruins of the Forum, cicadas whirring, lizards
scuttling, and Bilibin happily poking about just out of
earshot.

'Forget it, laddie! I said a lot o' things that night.
Maybe I was elated, meeting an old friend. I took a drop
too much brandy.'

'But you couldn't have made it up, sir! About Pio
Nono asking the foreign armies to march on Rome——'

'Sh, laddie!' MacWhirter gripped his arm in a tor-
turer's clutch and spoke earnestly in his ear. 'I'll tell you.
I wasn't making anything up. But look at Jonathan
Bilibin yonder, bless his good simple soul — would you
say he was happy?'

Mark laughed. 'Rather! He's in his element.'

'Then why spoil it? This is what he's dreamed of all
his life. He's a poor man. He'd never have seen all this
but for your grandmother.'

'I s'pose not, sir.'

MacWhirter thrust Mark away at arm's length and
scowled at him from under his tawny eyebrows. 'I don't
care a brass farthing whether *you* learn the difference
between a bath and a basilica — and I don't think you

much care yourself — but I'll not say another word to rob old Bilibin of his one great chance.'

'So . . . there *is* danger?'

'Danger? Och, no! There's no danger to English visitors anyhow. And ten to one nothing will happen for a month or two. By then you'll have journeyed on to Pompeii or somewhere. But you know old Bilibin. He's so conscientious, it almost hurts to look at him.' Mark laughed again, but MacWhirter's expression stopped him. 'I know I pull the old chap's leg — but he's a fine man, and don't you forget it.'

'No, sir.'

'If he'd only to think of himself, wild horses wouldn't drag him away from these chunks of marble. But he feels responsible for you, laddie, a helpless innocent boy.' MacWhirter's croaking chuckle, full of disbelief, gave Mark the uncomfortable feeling that the Scotsman already knew more about his character than Bilibin would learn in years. 'If he thought there was the least risk of any guns going off, he'd think it his duty to whisk you away somewhere else. Though it would be quite unnecessary.'

'But that's what he'd do,' Mark agreed.

'So we'll say no more on the subject?'

'Not a word, sir.' Mark had no desire to frighten Bilibin away from Rome. It would only mean going to some dead-alive spot where there would be just as many ruins but no MacWhirter, no city bustle, no hope of other amusement.

The tutor was walking back towards them, guide-book open, eyes shining, face transfigured.

'When one thinks of all the violent scenes this spot has witnessed,' he cried, 'how blessedly peaceful it all is today!'

Mark was surprised when MacWhirter suggested an evening visit to the Colosseum. They had already spent a morning there, dustily scrambling over the sun-baked shell of the gigantic amphitheatre.

'Och, no, this is different! This is a *festa* to celebrate the traditional foundation of the city——'

'753 B.C.,' said Bilibin automatically.

'I'll not contradict you! Anyhow, a Roman *festa* is something not to be missed. Bands, parades, fireworks, illuminations — and the grand climax a mass demonstration in the Colosseum itself.' As Bilibin hesitated, he went on with a wink at Mark: 'It'll be worth going, if only to give the laddie a notion of the place full of people, the way it must have looked when they had the gladiators.'

Bilibin needed no further persuading, and as the April twilight gathered on the following evening they joined the vast throng streaming through the arched entrances. Thousands of people were already clambering up the steep sides and ranging themselves, tier upon tier, until they seemed to hang there like an immense swarm of bees, darkly rippling and giving out an incessant buzz. As the three friends settled themselves into their places a band marched into the arena below. Mark recognized the tune Pietro had played.

'*Fratelli d'Italia!*'

'Correct, laddie. The *Marseillaise* of the Italian

E   55

revolution. And d'ye know, the young fellow who wrote it, Mameli, is only twenty-one?'

'Even the boys here seem mad on politics!'

'Ridiculous,' said Bilibin. 'They should give their minds to their studies. Prepare themselves for life.'

'Rome's not Eton,' MacWhirter retorted. 'Maybe it's the politics will decide the sort of life they'll have.'

'Oh, look!' Mark interrupted.

On some unnoticed signal hundreds of red-shaded lamps had been unmasked all round the base of the amphitheatre, so that the musicians in the centre were bathed in a crimson glow. A few moments later a broad green band ran round the middle rows, and finally, high above, the topmost tiers and arches were dramatically picked out in a cold white light.

'Stunning!' said Mark.

Bilibin regretted the choice of green. It made that section of the audience look like corpses.

'But these are the national colours,' MacWhirter explained, 'like the French red, white and blue.'

'There *is* no Italian nation——'

'Sh, man! Unless you want them to throw you down there like a Christian to the lions.' MacWhirter lowered his voice. 'They think they're *making* a nation.' He pointed down at the front row reserved for the leaders of the government. 'Yon's the man who'll do it, if anyone can.'

Even at that distance Mark recognized the great forehead and trim dark beard from MacWhirter's sketch.

'Mazzini, sir?'

'Correct. What he says, goes. He's one of the three Triumvirs running the republic. But the other two don't count for much.'

Bilibin said disapprovingly: 'I have read that the man is a Socialist, a Communist even——'

'Blether!'

'But, my dear MacWhirter——'

'Blether! Read his policy. *"No class-war, no unjust violation of property-rights, only a constant effort to improve the conditions of the less fortunate classes."* If he's got a fault, it's being too soft. He's an idealist. He makes a moral appeal to men's better natures.'

'I am relieved to hear it.'

'Ay — but what happens if they don't respond? He won't force them, he *has* no force. He's like a man riding bareback. The question is, can he stick on?'

Mark thought that the artist was unduly gloomy. As the programme of patriotic songs and speeches continued, it was obvious from the crowd's enthusiasm that Rome was solidly behind the gentle Mazzini.

Mark's own enthusiasm was rather less. Long speeches seemed twice as long in a language he did not understand. Bilibin also became restive, and peered at his watch in the pale lamplight, but the audience was too closely packed for them to escape before the end. 'Anyway, sir,' he could not help whispering to his tutor, 'it gives you a very good idea of what it must have been like for the Roman senators listening to Cicero!' Bilibin was not amused.

At last it was all over and they began to edge their way out with the others, stiff and numb from the hard seating. Shuffling along a few steps at a time, Mark suddenly saw a familiar head in front.

'Pietro!'

Pietro turned, his smile flashing as brightly as his spectacles.

'Why — Marco!'

'Fancy meeting in a crush like this!'

Mark wormed his way forward. When he reached Pietro he saw that Tessa was there too, overshadowed by the taller figures around her.

'Wasn't it wonderful?' she demanded. 'You enjoyed, yes?'

'Er — yes. Very much.'

The crowd pressed them forward together, chattering as they groped their way down the age-worn stairs in the uncertain light.

'What are you doing, Pietro? Have you found work?'

The youth hesitated. 'Not yet, not regular work. It — it is difficult now.'

'I tell him,' said Tessa, 'he should give English lessons. Many wish to learn.'

Her brother laughed. 'But few can pay! Don't worry. I shall find something.'

MacWhirter overtook them. Bilibin, too polite to push, was far behind. Mark introduced his friends. The towering Scotsman and the petite Italian girl took to each other immediately and went forging ahead. Mark and Pietro went more slowly, and, as they gained the open piazza below, a breathless Bilibin managed to reach their side.

'Mark — my dear boy — I thought I had lost you! Where is Mr. MacWhirter?'

'He's just in front, sir. Please, sir, this is Pietro Palma — you know, sir, my friend on the steamer. Pietro, this is my tutor, Mr. Bilibin.'

Pietro bowed. 'I am honoured, sir.'

Bilibin looked gratified. Mark had a sudden idea. If Pietro could teach English to Italians, why shouldn't he teach Italian to Englishmen?

'Pietro is a language-teacher,' he said quickly. 'You know, sir, Mr. MacWhirter said I ought to take some lessons——'

But Bilibin was on his guard at once. 'I should not like your Latin and Greek to suffer. There is Oxford to think of. Though no doubt a little Italian is quite a gentlemanly accomplishment . . .' He smiled kindly at Pietro — Bilibin could never be anything but kind. 'I must consider the matter, Mr. — er — Mr. Palma. If you would care to give me your card?'

Pietro looked embarrassed. Mark rushed to the rescue. 'Pietro has not had time yet to get cards——'

'Of course! Then if I might inscribe your address, sir, in my little note-book?'

Pietro seemed curiously unwilling to give his address. 'I should be most happy to call on the *signore*,' he mumbled, 'when he has had leisure to consider the matter——'

'It will be better if I have your address,' said Bilibin with unusual firmness.

I know, thought Mark gloomily, he doesn't mean me to spend any time on Italian, but he doesn't want Pietro coming round to our lodgings — he'd sooner send a polite letter saying 'no'.

Pietro reluctantly gave an address which Bilibin pencilled into his note-book — and Mark took pains to memorise. At that moment MacWhirter and Tessa reappeared, and from the way Bilibin opened his eyes Mark felt more than ever certain that his friendship with the young Italians would not be encouraged.

'You are sure you can amuse yourself? You will be all right?' Bilibin inquired anxiously for the third time.

'Of course, sir,' Mark assured him patiently.

The chance he wanted had come within two days of his encounter with the Palmas. Bilibin had been invited to an afternoon gathering of the English colony in Rome, a strictly grown-up affair. As a bachelor and a clergyman, Bilibin seemed in great demand by the good ladies of his native country, and for once he had been tempted to take a few hours' freedom from his duties.

'I expect Miss Ellis will be there,' Mark added innocently, and was delighted to see the blush rising in his tutor's cheeks.

As soon as Bilibin was safely on his way, Mark walked down into the piazza and jumped into a cab. 'Via Caterina,' he ordered, adding the number which he had remembered to look up in Italian and pronouncing it as confidently as he could: '*Ventidue!*'

The driver raised a shaggy eyebrow. '*Trastevere!*' he remarked in a somewhat shocked tone.

'*Tras——? Ah, si, si!*'

Just in time Mark recognized 'Trastevere' as the name of the unfashionable western district on the opposite side of the Tiber. He jingled the money in his trouser-pocket in case the man thought he had not the fare for so long a drive. The driver shrugged his shoulders as if to show that he was taking no responsibility, flicked his bony horse, and started off.

When they crossed the Ponte Sisto and entered the slums beyond, Mark understood the man's hesitation and felt thankful that Bilibin knew nothing of the expedition. Here was a Rome very different from the tourists' area round the Piazza di Spagna. Crumbling tenements, neglected for generations, leant dangerously across tenebrous alleys. Ragged, fly-blown babies rolled in the dust, uncouth women screeched from balconies, unshaven and villainous-looking men muttered in black doorways.

Mark found that his hands felt moist with more than the heat of the late April sunshine. This was a sinister neighbourhood where anything might happen. He began almost to wish that he had not come. Then, to his relief, the cab turned a corner and began to climb a slightly more respectable street. It halted at No. 22, a house which had seen better days but was not actually repellent.

The driver seemed to be demanding a fantastic sum, about ten times as much as Mark had ever seen Mac-Whirter pay for the longest journey. The man was becoming abusive and Mark was secretly getting frightened when, to his joy, an incredulous Pietro appeared at his elbow and settled the argument with a few furious phrases.

'Marco! You should not have come here! This is a dreadful district!'

'Oh, it's rather interesting,' said Mark airily, his courage restored.

Pietro took him up several flights of uncarpeted stairs into a room which was small and bare but clean and almost attractive after the squalor through which he had come. A cheap print of Mazzini adorned the cracked plaster wall. Mark checked a smile. At home or abroad, he could never get away from other people's hero-worshipping.

'You will excuse my bed? We have only the two rooms.' He opened the door again and called: 'Tessa!'

'*Momento!*'

It was rather more than a moment before his sister appeared. She was carrying a tray with small cups of strong, fragrant coffee and some tiny cakes. She looked pleased but not surprised.

'I looked down from my window,' she explained. 'I saw it was Marco.' She put out her hand. 'Welcome to our disreputable home! It is not often a cab stops at this address, so every head pops out.'

An hour passed like lightning as they exchanged news, chattering and laughing and interrupting each other. It was good to be with young people again. Pietro and Tessa were so gay, though Mark guessed, reading between the lines, that things were not going too well with them. They had met with a cool welcome from their uncle, who hated the new Republic and was horrified by their views. All would be well, Pietro insisted, when the government got into its stride. There would be work for everybody. Next year, perhaps, they would start to build railways. Meanwhile things were difficult, but he would earn a living somehow, and Tessa would help.

'What is the time?' the girl asked suddenly. 'Your Mr. Bilibin will not be having a heart-attack?'

'Not on my account.' Mark giggled. 'I don't know about his adored Miss Ellis.' He explained his tutor's new interest. Tessa was much intrigued. Though she had grown up in London she still thought it funny that the priests of other churches were allowed to marry.

'I'm all right till six o'clock,' said Mark.

'I'll see you safely as far as the bridge,' Pietro promised.

'I have a better idea, Pietro! Let us all get out of this hot attic and take a little country walk outside the walls. Perhaps we could find a pleasanter way home for Marco?'

A steep lane, overshadowed by the garden-walls of decayed mansions, brought them to the Porta San Pancrazio, a narrow arched opening in the massive seventeenth-century fortifications protecting this side of Rome. Beyond rolled a landscape of trees and terraced vineyards, with here and there a majestic villa embowered in its private grounds. A brother-and-sister argument developed as Pietro tried to point out the various landmarks. Mark settled it by bringing out the plan of the city which Bilibin had bought in London.

'This is fine,' said Pietro. 'We can walk through the Corsini gardens and the Pamfili, then we can cut through those vineyards till we strike the road from Civita-vecchia——'

'And come in again through the Porta Pertusa!' cried Tessa. 'We have never been that way ourselves. Can you find your own way home, Marco, if we take you as far as Sant' Angelo?'

'Easily!'

'*Avanti!*'

At first their way continued uphill, for the city-walls, somewhat surprisingly, did not mark the crest of the Janiculum, which still sloped up in front of them to the lofty Villa Corsini on the skyline. It was also known, said Pietro, as 'The House of the Four Winds', and in rough weather it would deserve the name.

Today, though, on this soft afternoon in the late Roman spring-time, few country-walks could have been pleasanter. They went up the drive between the trim box-hedges, past the mansion itself and a garden-wall topped with small orange-trees in pots, down into a shady little valley with a stream at the bottom, and up the other side into the even more spacious grounds of the Villa Pamfili with their rose-gardens and evergreen avenues.

'Now we must find a way down into that lane,' said Pietro, pointing into the depths below the terraces. 'Can you manage, Tessa?'

'Of course, silly!'

Careless of her skirt — and sometimes, thought Mark, even careless of her neck — Tessa followed her brother in a rough scramble down through the shadowy foliage. It was a dizzy descent. Mark bit his lip when, at one point, he found himself peering down a sheer wall into the lane they wanted to reach, but after a little questing about Pietro discovered a ruinous part where they could lower themselves by degrees, helped by branches. It was scaring but not actually suicidal. Grandmother would never have approved. Nor would Bilibin — even though they found an ancient aqueduct bordering the lane on the other side.

Pietro and Tessa, however, had no desire to discuss classical Rome. What was almost as bad, from Mark's point of view, they began talking about the patriotic rally and their wonderful Mazzini. What did Marco's friends think of him? Mark tried to be tactful.

'Mr. MacWhirter says he's a great idealist——'

'Of course!'

'But is he practical enough?'

'How not?' demanded Tessa furiously.

'I — I don't know. But hasn't he started revolutions before, and they've failed because there weren't enough men and guns, and the people who followed him have been shot or put in prison——'

'Every great movement must have its martyrs,' said Pietro. 'If you knew Mazzini as we do——'

'Well, of course, I don't——'

'Pietro!' Tessa clutched his sleeve, vehement as always. 'We could take Marco to see him. Tomorrow, when we go!'

'Here, I say, you don't mean it?'

'Why not? We can take you — if Mr. Bilibin will allow!'

'Oh, I can manage old Bilibin — for a thing like that,' said Mark confidently. It would be interesting, quite an honour in fact, to see this famous character at close quarters. Even Bilibin would have to admit that.

The walk took longer than they had expected, for, though the map showed the distance as little more than a mile, they had to trace a zigzag route down one hillside, over a stream, and then uphill again. At last they came out on the very road by which Mark had driven into Rome the first evening. The ramparts of the Vatican Hill rose straight in front of them, but there was no sign of the gate promised on their map.

Mark looked anxiously at his watch. It would never do to be late home. A cart was creaking towards them, its driver drowsing over his pair of milk-white oxen. Pietro hailed him. He woke, laughed, and pointed to a particularly blank stretch of the fortifications in front of them. Pietro clucked with annoyance.

'He says that the Porta Pertusa was bricked up years ago! And still the map shows it! That is Roman inefficiency — that is what we have to alter.'

In the end it made little difference. They trudged along parallel with the wall and went in by the Porta Cavalleggieri, which was on the direct line for Mark's lodgings. His friends put him in a cab in front of St. Peter's, telling him firmly, in the driver's hearing, exactly how much to pay. He reached home just ten minutes ahead of his tutor.

'I met Pietro,' he explained cautiously as they sat down to their meal. 'He's calling for me tomorrow afternoon — he's offered to take me into the Quirinal Palace and introduce me to Mr. Mazzini. Will that be all right, sir?'

Bilibin did not answer for so long that Mark grew worried till he realised that his tutor was not considering his request at all but was far away in some agreeable dream of his own.

'Will that be all right, sir?' he repeated.

'Of course, of course. Very nice,' said Bilibin mechanically.

But whether it was Mark's meeting with Mazzini that would be 'very nice', or some quite different programme, Mark was by no means sure.

The palace was only a short walk from the lodgings. It stood on a hill and looked out over a vast square, which made Mark feel smaller than usual. It was a stately building in the ponderous foreign style he now knew to be baroque. In the ordinary way it was where the Pope lived.

Pietro and Tessa had paid two previous visits to their father's old friend and they were quite undismayed by all this magnificence. They led the way boldly inside, up the grand staircase to the gallery, and then along corridors in which Mark's footsteps seemed alarmingly loud. There were soldiers and servants and secretaries bustling to and fro, but nobody tried to stop them.

'He has no bodyguard,' Tessa explained.

'He is too trusting,' said her brother. 'That could be dangerous.'

'He lives just as he did when he was a poor exile in London, Marco! He is the most important man in this palace, but he has chosen such a simple little room — but here we are, you will see for yourself.'

Pietro knocked on a door. A voice called, 'Come in,' and there was Mazzini coming round his writing-table to welcome them, his massive head thrust forward, his hand outstretched. He did not look very heroic in his shabby frock-coat. But for the beard and the silk hand-kerchief knotted at his throat — couldn't he afford clean collars, Mark wondered? — he would have passed for a lawyer's clerk at home. But then Pietro had already said how little the man cared for outward show. As Triumvir of the Roman Republic he received the equivalent of eight English pounds a week, but most of that he gave away to people in need. At dinner-time he walked out to a cheap restaurant near by.

'And this is our English friend, Mark Apperley——'

Mark felt his hand pressed rather than shaken.

Mazzini's eyes were extraordinary — dark, penetrating, with a power that was surprising in so gentle and kindly a face. When he spoke, too, Mark understood why he had cast a spell over so many people.

'From England? Ah, my second home!' He told Mark how unhappy he had been when he had first settled in London, how he had hated the strangeness and the lack of sun, but how he had come gradually to love even the fog. 'And now I have many friends in England. So, I think, has Italy. Not perhaps all your newspapers.' He smiled grimly. 'Your *Times* calls us "the degenerate remnant of the Roman people". We shall see.'

Mark looked round the room with curiosity. This was an experience to remember. Mazzini followed his gaze to a jar of red and white tulips which, with some foliage, made a splash of patriotic colour against the plain wall.

'Ah, my flowers! Someone sends me flowers every day, I have no idea who. ⌊I must have a secret admirer.'

'You have a million admirers!' cried Pietro. 'And they are not all secret!'

Mazzini waved away the compliment with his sensitive hands. Mark felt embarrassed for him, but perhaps, being Italian, Mazzini could stand that sort of remark better than an Englishman. Tessa ran to the corner of the room and picked up a guitar.

'Play us a tune, Mr. Mazzini!'

'No, no, Teresa!' He turned to Mark with a smile. 'She teases me. Only when I am alone do I play. At night, in here, when all the meetings are over and all the papers are signed, when there is nobody to hear the noise I make.'

There was a tap on the door and a secretary entered holding out a dispatch. Mazzini broke the seal and unfolded the paper. As he read it his face changed. He broke into a flood of Italian. Mark caught one familiar name. Civitavecchia. Pietro and Tessa were wide-eyed with alarm.

The secretary rushed out again. Mazzini turned to his visitors and relapsed into English.

'I am sorry, my young friends, I shall have to go now. Something serious has happened.'

They found themselves walking away through the

long corridors. Mark whispered: 'I say, did you understand what it was all about?'

'Yes,' said Pietro grimly. 'The French are landing an
army at Civitavecchia. They are going to march on
Rome and overthrow the Republic.'

F

Chapter Six

THE MAN ON THE WHITE HORSE

'So France has won the race.' MacWhirter sprawled contentedly on the sofa. 'While the Austrians are mopping up the North — while the Spaniards and Neapolitans twiddle their thumbs — the enterprising French have filled a few steamers with their soldiers, and *voilà*!'

Mark was nettled by his tone. Pietro and Tessa had been so shattered by this news. They could have understood any of the other foreign powers working to destroy the Roman Republic. They were all tyrannies, Pietro said, all natural enemies of freedom. But France was herself a republic. To use her forces against the people of Italy was a betrayal.

'I suppose it's all the same to you, sir?' Mark could not keep a slight edge of hostility out of his voice.

'Absolutely.' MacWhirter grinned annoyingly. 'I am a journalist. I'm interested solely in the news.'

Bilibin came in, looking flustered.

'If the laundry-woman does not bring back our clean linen tonight,' he announced solemnly, 'I fear that we shall have to abandon it. But I feel sure that your grandmother will excuse the sacrifice of a few shirts in a situation like——'

'Bilibin! What on earth are you blethering about?'

'Mark's safety is my first responsibility. You, of course, have a duty to your employers, you cannot leave Rome——'

'Are *you* planning to?' MacWhirter cackled. Mark stared aghast. This was news to him.

The clergyman blinked. 'Naturally! If there is to be fighting——'

'There'll be no fighting, man. The French have landed eight thousand troops, as good as any in Europe. What can Mazzini put against them? The old Papal Carabinieri — can he expect them to die for the Republic? The new National Guard — a mixed bunch of amateurs? A few hundred volunteers from other parts of Italy?'

'But — but — there's talk of resistance to the death!'

'The Romans are good at talking. There'll be a few shots maybe — just for appearance' sake. Then there'll be an honourable surrender, the French will move in, and the next morning it will be business as usual.'

'You really think so?'

'I saw the British Consul an hour ago. The official advice is, don't leave the city.'

Bilibin brightened. 'In view of that, perhaps——'

'Anyhow, where would you take the boy if you went?'

'Where?'

'You can hardly go back to Civitavecchia, straight into the arms of the advancing French. Wherever else you drive, north, south, east or west, you'll find chaos. Mazzini can keep order in Rome, but it's very different outside. What with rebels and irregulars and plain brigands — not to mention the Spanish and Neapolitan troops, whose notion of discipline is rather eccentric! — I think Grandma Apperley would prefer her precious laddie to stay here, not risk the manifold hazards of the open road.'

'Oh, yes, sir,' said Mark. 'I'm sure Grandmother would expect us to stay.'

'Very well then. *I* have no desire to leave Rome,' said Bilibin. 'I was merely anxious not to let my own selfish interests—— '

'Your interest in antiquities?' said MacWhirter, with a sly glance at Mark.

'Exactly,' said Bilibin with dignity.

'Don't fash yourself. You're doing the sensible thing. And you won't have to lose your laundry, either.'

'But of course we shall fight,' said Pietro quietly.

'He was drilling for two hours this morning,' Tessa added with pride.

They had turned up at Mark's lodgings early the next afternoon. Pietro's shabby blue uniform hung loosely on his narrow shoulders. He had joined the Student Corps. There were nearly three hundred of them, he said, mostly from the University or the art schools, though no fussy questions were asked. If you wanted to fight for Italy, that was enough.

Bilibin took this sudden invasion of the sitting-room very well, even though it included an attractive girl. The timetable was scrapped, anyhow. Who could study when blaring bands and hysterical processions marched incessantly beneath the windows? And now, to complete the uproar, in danced MacWhirter, seething with laughter and flaunting a huge Union Jack like a bull-fighter's cape.

'You're to hang this from your balcony when th French march in!'

'The French will never march in!' cried Tessa. Her earrings swung and shook with her emotion.

'And who'll stop 'em, lassie? Apart from your gallant brother?'

'Garibaldi will stop them!'

'Garibaldi?' MacWhirter's manner changed. In a moment he was the alert journalist. 'He's miles away. He's watching the Neapolitans.'

'Not now, sir,' said Pietro. 'He enters Rome this afternoon. That's why we came for Marco. He should see the entry of Garibaldi and the Legion.'

'So should I, by Jove! Or my editor will have something to say. Get your hat, Bilibin. We've only to walk the length of the street, they'll have to come along the Corso—— '

'But—— '

'No but about it! This is news. Where's my sketch-book? Come on.'

He bustled them all downstairs. They had almost to run, Tessa especially, as he stalked along the sun-drenched pavement. At the corner they came up against a baffling wall of solid humanity. MacWhirter prised a gap with his hefty shoulder, flashed a coin — and in no time a shopkeeper was ushering them up to a balcony, from which they could look straight along the Corso into the hazy distance at the city's northern gate.

'A chair!' ordered MacWhirter. 'And Heaven help anyone who jogs my elbow!' He began sketching the long perspective, the fuzz of faces, the streaming tricolour flags, the rooftop watchers crouched upon the red-brown tiles. As his pencil swept to and fro his tongue hardly slackened.

'Garibaldi's the one man who might do something. Extraordinary fellow. Piedmontese. Started as a ship's captain — met Mazzini — went political. Born fighter — been in South America — fought in all sorts of revolutions. Irregular — what the Spaniards call a guerrilla. Made rings round the Austrians in Lombardy last year. Hit-and-run stuff, here-today-and-gone-tomorrow. Don't quite see him in a siege——'

'He will save Rome,' cried Tessa. 'Everyone believes that.'

'Then everyone must believe in miracles, lassie.'

Mark broke in tactfully: 'I think something's happening, sir——'

'He's coming!' Tessa leant out so excitedly that Mark laid a hand on her arm.

There was a faint murmur, half a mile away, near the Porta del Popolo. Still the road stretched empty but expectant into the distance. The murmur grew. It was like fire creeping along a dry hedge. The kerbside multitudes rustled, swayed, then roared into life. Suddenly the

roadway was empty no longer, it was speckled with steadily advancing dots of colour. The cheers rose deafeningly.

'*Evviva Garibaldi!*'

'The man on the white horse!' Tessa shouted in Mark's ear.

'You knocked my arm!' howled MacWhirter.

Mark saw a big man, barrel-chested, with a reddish-golden beard and a face like a lion's, broad-muzzled, t awny from sun and wind. He wore a loose red tunic, almost a shirt, and a strange white cloak.

'His old South American get-up!' MacWhirter was sketching frenziedly. 'The cloak is a cowboy's *poncho*. Note the cowboy saddle too. Those black plumes in his hat are ostrich-feathers — all those with black plumes and red shirts were with him in Uruguay. Sort of uniform.'

Behind the general rode an immense negro. Everything about him was dark, from his blue *poncho* to the black horse which contrasted so effectively with Garibaldi's beautiful white charger.

'Aguyar — Garibaldi's shadow. See the lasso coiled up on his saddle? He was a horse-breaker once. Parents were both slaves.'

Odd, thought Mark — a negro from the pampas here in Rome to defend Italian liberty! It must be a powerful spell that Garibaldi cast over his followers. Among the red-shirted figures MacWhirter pointed out Ugo Bassi, the friar who had joined the Legion as its chaplain but had thrown in his lot with them completely.

'Like Friar Tuck and Robin Hood?' suggested Mark.

'They *look* more like a gang of outlaws than a regiment,' said Bilibin with a sniff.

There was a tiny detachment of cavalry with red fezzes and long lances flashing in the sun, but the rank and file of the Legion trudged by in dark blue tunics and wide-brimmed black hats, muskets or pikes on their shoulders and murderous-looking daggers in their belts. MacWhirter's lips moved silently. When the tail of the column had passed he said:

'Must be a thousand of them. All the same, it's not enough.'

They saw a good deal of the legionaries in the next few days. The men were billeted in the near-by Convent of San Silvestro and the general himself took up quarters in the Via della Carozze near the Spanish Steps. He became a familiar figure. Almost always the curly-bearded negro was at his heels.

Two days later another column of troops was welcomed into the excited city. These were much more to Bilibin's taste. They were the six hundred gentlemen-volunteers of the Lombard Bersaglieri, disciplined soldiers, immaculate in dark green uniforms, with cock's feathers in their hats and the Cross of Savoy on their belts. They were fugitives from the Austrian territories. Their hopes lay in the Kingdom of Piedmont, whose uniform they imitated. It was only because the defeated Piedmontese dared not shelter them any longer that they had come south to Rome as the next best thing.

'Unfortunately,' said MacWhirter, 'they have come too late.'

'How do you mean, sir?' Mark was puzzled. The

siege had not opened, barricades and trenches were still being made everywhere, the French had not moved from their base on the coast.

MacWhirter explained. 'They were stopped by the French when they landed. General Oudinot let them pass on one condition — that they would take no part in any hostilities until after May the fourth. They gave their word of honour and I think they'll keep it.'

'It's the twenty-ninth of April today——'

'Precisely. And Oudinot must be ready to strike. He must have reckoned that it will be all over by the fourth of May.'

Things began to happen, in fact, the very next day. MacWhirter burst in upon them at breakfast.

'It's started — the French have been sighted. There isn't *that* much hurry,' he added with a laugh as Bilibin sprang to his feet and upset his coffee-cup. 'They're still miles away. You can finish your meal. You'll still see everything.'

'S-see everything?' Bilibin was fumbling agitatedly with the Union Jack on the balcony. Suddenly it escaped his grasp and went flopping over into the street, where it engulfed an elderly priest who was passing beneath. Mark clattered downstairs to apologize and bring it back. When he returned, MacWhirter was saying:

'You'll be safe enough on the hill behind here — everyone's congregating there to watch. But it's too far away for me. I'm off across the river. Garibaldi's on the Janiculum — that's the place for a ringside seat.'

Mark let the flag droop limply over the sofa. The Janiculum Hill was where the Palmas lived. Pietro would be with the Student Corps. Tessa oughtn't to be alone.

'Mr. MacWhirter——'

But the Scot had gone.

'Help me with this flag,' said Bilibin.

Together they draped it over the balcony. The morning was loud with clanging bells and tapping drums. Shrill voices tossed the latest rumours from window to window.

'There,' said Bilibin. 'That should protect us from annoyance when the French march in.'

'Can we go and watch, sir?'

Bilibin hesitated. 'Watch? H'm . . .'

'Mr. MacWhirter said everyone was going up on the Pincian Hill. There can't be any danger. The French are still miles away — and there's all the city and the river between. I expect,' Mark added wickedly, 'that Miss Ellis and her mother will be there.'

'H'm, yes . . . well, perhaps it would be best just to go up and get some notion of what is happening.' Bilibin dusted his top-hat with his usual care and led the way downstairs.

As MacWhirter had told them, all the foreign visitors were streaming up the Spanish Steps to the public gardens on the Pincian Hill. The excited chatter, the parasols, the billowing dresses and the flashing telescopes suggested a race-meeting rather than a battle. Bilibin had no sooner replaced his hat after bowing to one lady than he was raising it to another.

'What a crowd!' he panted. 'Mark, my boy——'

'Sir?'

'If we should get separated——'

'Yes, sir?'

'We shall meet again at the apartments. But be careful — don't get lost——'

'Rather not, sir!'

Mark took this as an invitation to make himself scarce. Bilibin was climbing purposefully towards the bewitching figure of Miss Ellis, whom, with a cluster of other ladies, he had just observed on the skyline.

Looking back across the rooftops of the city, with the Tiber winding through the middle, Mark saw that the Pincian Hill, however handy for the tourist quarter, was not a good place from which to see the French advance. It was safe simply because it stood at the north-east corner of Rome and the French were coming from the west. But the whole city, climbing the slopes of the Janiculum and Vatican Hills to the western fortifications, lay between the gossiping sightseers and any excitement that was likely to develop.

He doubled back. Down through the gardens, down the marble swirl of the Spanish Steps, across the piazza to the cab-rank. He was glad that it was not the same driver today.

It was a long roundabout journey. They were held up by a marching column of Carabinieri. Several times they had to make a detour to avoid barricades. Finally, at the bottom of the Palmas' street, the man refused to go further. Mark jumped out, handed him the proper fare, and cut short his voluble cursing by running up the road. He was breathless when he reached the top landing of the house. Neither door opened to his knocking.

A woman appeared downstairs and called something. He ran down. She made signs. The *signorino*? She raised an imaginary musket and shot several invisible Frenchmen. The *signorina*? She drew Mark to the doorstep and pointed uphill.

'Porta San Pancrazio!'

'*Grazie, signora*——'

'*Prego!*' She smiled and nodded. He hurried off.

To his surprise the gate was still open, though there were guards with fixed bayonets. One challenged him. '*Ingles*,' said Mark, putting on a show of confidence worthy of his grandmother.

'*Ingles?*' The bronze face broke into a smile of understanding. Beckoning Mark through the archway the sentry pointed up the road beyond. Fifty yards away MacWhirter was sitting on a tree-stump. Tessa stood beside him.

The artist, intent on sketching, welcomed him with a growl. 'Perhaps you can keep the lassie quiet. Keeps blethering about her precious brother. I tell her he's all right——'

'I am perfectly calm!' Tessa retorted. Every nerve in her body quivered.

'I thought the gate would be shut,' said Mark.

'What's the sense, laddie?' MacWhirter pointed his pencil at the Villa Corsini on its hill in front. 'Yon house is the key to this position. If the French capture that, their guns will command the gate.'

'Where *are* the French, sir?'

'No sign yet. Take a peek through my telescope.'

Mark focussed it eagerly and the countryside over which he had walked a few days earlier leapt into sharp detail. From where he was standing the wall ran north along the Janiculum Hill, a brick-faced cliff above a sea of greenery. After a mile it thrust outwards at right-angles, enclosing the Vatican Hill like a promontory. As he swung the telescope slowly to the left, past St. Peter's dome and the ancient round tower and the very end of the salient ramparts, he let out a sharp cry.

'There they are, sir!'

A blue centipede with bright red legs was creeping up the road from Civitavecchia.

'Let me see!' MacWhirter glared through the telescope and snorted. 'I told you, lassie. They're not coming our way at all. They're taking the normal route. I wonder if Mazzini's changed his mind.'

'Changed his mind?' asked Tessa suspiciously.

'About resisting.'

'Never!'

'Well, the French don't look as if they're expecting any trouble. Their scouts are sauntering along only a few yards in front of the column——'

Poom!

The noise went rolling across the landscape. Mark saw a wisp of smoke curling from the Vatican ramparts. As he watched, a denser cloud gushed from an embrasure near it. A second cannon-shot echoed away to the distant hills.

'I told you!' cried Tessa.

Even without the telescope they could see that the French column had halted. Gun-teams were streaking forward from the rear, wheeling and unlimbering beside the road. Musketry crackled. The French field-guns began to bang away. Tawny clouds of brick-dust fanned up from the walls.

Mark felt an odd excitement. His pulse raced. He was watching real war, men shooting at each other to kill — though at this distance they looked more like toy soldiers miraculously come to life, a nursery dream. Mac-Whirter, who had reported several campaigns, was actually laughing.

'A lot of use, those pop-guns! They should have brought heavy stuff. Siege-artillery. They didn't reckon on this.'

'A shock for them!' said Tessa gleefully.

'Can't understand it, though. Take a peek, laddie. See the way they're facing? They're half a mile short of the gate. There's no way in there.'

Mark laughed as the powerful lens revealed the explanation. 'What a lark, sir! They've done what we did the other afternoon — they're using an old map that shows the Porta Pertusa. They were planning to march in through a gate that isn't there!'

MacWhirter snorted, snatched back the telescope, then grunted amused agreement. 'You've hit it, laddie. Here, hold this while I make some notes. Half past eleven. French assault on non-existent gateway. H'm. They'll have to think again.'

'They are, sir. They're moving along the road now.'

The firing was continuous. The whole length of the Vatican wall flashed and spurted with smoke. As Mark remembered, it was half a mile from the bricked-up gateway to the nearest usable entrance, and every yard of the road was under hot fire from the parallel ramparts overlooking it.

'Oudinot's been over-confident. No siege-guns, no scaling ladders, no reconnaissance — and even now he's marching his troops across the front of the enemy! Lucky for him he's not up against a real army.' MacWhirter was talking more to himself than to his companions. Mark took the chance to whisper:

'Where's your brother?'

Tessa pointed. 'They marched out that way. I think they're posted somewhere in the Pamfili gardens — you know, where we were the other afternoon?'

'I'm not likely to forget scrambling down that awful wall!'

'Look — isn't that Garibaldi?'

The general had appeared on the terrace of the Villa Corsini. Among the cluster of red shirts they could also make out the tall negro. The legionaries were watching the distant enemy as intently as they were themselves.

'Aching to be in the fight,' said MacWhirter.

Tessa's fingers were twisting nervously. In a low voice she confessed to Mark: 'I am torn in two pieces. One part is glad the French have not come this way — but the other part of me is ashamed to be glad.'

'I know.'

'Do you?'

'You can't help being glad that Pietro isn't in danger.'

'That is it. Pietro is brave. He does not really want to be a soldier, though, to fight and kill people. He wants to be an engineer, he wants to build bridges and railways. He is more quiet than I am, more peaceful——'

'So I've noticed!' Mark tried to make a joke of it. Tessa was upset. He wanted to lessen her tension.

'Pietro forces himself to do this because he knows it is his duty. But all the time he is longing for the day when it will be over and he can do his real work.'

The firing had slackened. The French seemed to have given up their attack on the Porta Cavallegieri, but they showed no sign of withdrawing. The red-and-blue figures, the gleaming cannon, the grey and chestnut horses, still dotted the green slopes.

MacWhirter shut his sketch-book. He had completed a panoramic impression of the scene, with squiggly indications of bursting shells and galloping gun-teams which later, in the quiet of his lodgings, he would work up for the benefit of the *Pictorial Chronicle*. He had sketched sentries, staff-officers, spectators. He had made a detailed drawing of the Villa Corsini.

'You never know,' he said darkly. 'May need it.'

'What'll happen now, sir?'

'Hard to say. The French can't get in and the Italians haven't the forces to come out and drive them off. I expect that's what Garibaldi would like to try, but he's no fool. Perhaps this young fellow can tell us something.'

He hailed an officer who was riding back towards the city. The Italian smiled, pointed towards the villa, shouted something, and passed on. Mark heard Tessa gasp. He saw she had gone pale. She was fingering the crucifix at her neck. She seemed to be praying.

'He says that Garibaldi's going to move out against them. The Student Corps have been given the honour of leading the way.' MacWhirter was frowning as he scribbled a few more lines in his note-book. 'I can't see from here. I'm going forward.' He stalked up the road. Tessa started after him and Mark followed her.

In a minute or two they reached a point from which they could look straight down the sunken lane at the foot of the Pamfili terraces. There was the high wall down which they themselves had clambered so dizzily. Now the students were slithering down, laughing as though they were out on a picnic. Mark felt a sudden longing to be with them. So many of them were scarcely older than himself. He sighed. Would it be his fate in life always to be out of things, always a spectator?

Silence fell as the amateur soldiers formed into ranks. They stood darkly shadowed by the overhanging trees of the Villa Pamfili and the arches of the ruined aqueduct on the other side of the lane.

MacWhirter grunted suddenly. 'Lord save us! Will ye look yonder?'

Up the same road, further away but more plainly visible in the full sunshine, they could see the glinting bayonets and tall shakoes of a French column steadily advancing upon the city.

It was an agonizing moment. Would the students see the enemy in time? The blue-and-red infantry came on. There was no sign of scouts in front. They could not yet have seen the students mustering in the dappled shade of the trees.

'This is fantastic,' said MacWhirter between his teeth.

They stood there on the crest of the hill, helpless and fascinated. Mark seized Tessa's hand, partly to comfort her, partly to make sure that she did not go racing wildly into danger.

In the dark hollow below them a bugle brayed. It was followed by a long-drawn, yelling sort of cheer, fraying out through the tense and quivering heat of the afternoon. The students were charging. The French files reeled and dissolved in ruin. The neat rows of slanted bayonets and glossy shakoes joggled and merged into the confused torrent of tossing plumes, of furiously brandished swords and muskets and pikes.

'They're too few,' groaned the artist.

Yet for a time it looked as though the Student Corps had achieved a miracle. The trained soldiers were swept back by the thoughtless courage of the young volunteers. Tessa, her fears forgotten, was almost hysterical with triumph. Mark kept a tight hold of her hand.

Discipline and numbers began to tell. The French surged forward again. Now the students were getting the worst of it. Some could be seen climbing back to the safety of the terraces, then turning to fire down through the leafy branches at their pursuers.

MacWhirter suddenly became aware of his companions. 'You'd best get out of here.'

'But, sir—— '

'Do as I say, Mark. Get the lassie out of here.'

It was not so easy. Tessa jerked her hand free. Her eyes were big with anguish.

'I cannot go. Pietro is down there—— '

Soldiers shouted at them. A messenger thundered by. Stones spurted in their faces — for an instant Mark thought that they were already under fire.

'Tessa, you must. It's dangerous here.'

'Go yourself, then. You do not understand.' She flung off the arm he put round her shoulders. 'This does not matter to you — you are English — you laugh at everything—— '

'I *do* understand. But there's nothing we can do. We're too young—— '

'*You* are too young! All right, go to your lesson-books, little English boy!'

He tried hard, afterwards, to forget those words. She had not known what she was saying. But the memory rankled for a long time.

MacWhirter had vanished. All round them were excited figures, sightseers racing for safety, reinforcements streaming out through the city gate. Suddenly Mark saw close at hand, towering above the tumult like a rock above the sea, Garibaldi on his white charger, his white *poncho* like a banner against the sky. In all that delirium Garibaldi's was the one calm face, serene as sculpture. Only his eyes glowed fiercely with emotion.

A strange thrill went through Mark. In that moment he had had a glimpse of something utterly outside his former experience. Perhaps — perhaps, in spite of all his resistance to Grandmother's family pride and Bilibin's reverence for the great men of antiquity and even the Palmas' rather tiresome enthusiasm for Mazzini, there *were* heroes in real life, men truly great, as great as they were made out to be in books?

But it was no moment for quiet thought. An officer shouted a question. Garibaldi answered briefly, wheeled his horse, and was gone, the giant negro galloping behind.

'What did he say, Tessa?'

'He just laughed and said, "You must follow my black plume".'

The sight of the General seemed to have calmed her. She let Mark lead her back inside the gate. They joined the anxious crowd lining the ramparts.

From there they heard and imagined, rather than saw, the life-and-death struggle for the strategic position outside. Wounded men limped back with ever-changing accounts of the battle. The French had occupied the Pamfili gardens — the students and the legionaries were holding out in this place and that — Garibaldi was preparing a counter-attack from the Villa Corsini — men were dying in heaps amid the rose-bushes — the good friar, Ugo Bassi, had been captured as he knelt beside them . . .

It was an hour of torturing suspense. Tessa peered down to scan the face of every wounded youth. Mark was thinking that, even though Pietro had not been carried in through the gate, he was just as likely to be lying in the trampled gardens or in the sunken lane.

At last the firing slackened. Bugles rang out from among the trees. The fighting seemed over — but who had won? A chorus of horror, almost panic, rose from the watching crowd as a column of red-trousered soldiers came marching up the road. It changed to howls of delight and derision when it was seen that the Frenchmen were unarmed and some of them bare-headed, and that they were being herded along by red-fezzed lancers and students.

Tessa screamed. 'There's Pietro!'

She started down a long ladder which offered the nearest, if not the safest, way down from the ramparts. Mark followed. They reached the gateway just as Pietro came through.

He grinned, dirty-faced, his spectacles askew. 'Can't stop — I'm on duty!' He passed on with the prisoners.

Tessa was gabbling her gratitude to the saints. She turned to Mark, radiant, relapsing into English. 'He's safe, Marco, he's safe!'

MacWhirter loomed beside them like a benign bear. 'Of course he's safe! What did I tell ye?'

'What's happened, sir?'

'Garibaldi's done it. The man's a marvel. The French are falling back. I doubt they'll stop this side of Civita-vecchia.'

'Oh dear,' said Mark, struck by a sudden thought. 'I'd better go back and make my peace with old Bilibin!'

SEVEN-DAY SOLDIER

No girl, thought Mark crossly the next afternoon,
ought to go on like that about a brother.
Pietro this, Pietro that . . . one might suppose that the heroic Pietro had routed the whole French
army single-handed!

Himself an only child, Mark had always found it a
little difficult to appreciate Tessa's feeling for her brother.
Much as he liked Pietro, he had sometimes felt a

slight irritation, which he now recognized as plain jealousy. Yesterday had widened the gulf between them. It was no longer just the difference of two or three years. It was the difference between a soldier and a schoolboy.

'Today, perhaps,' said Bilibin earnestly, 'we can revert to our normal routine.'

To him yesterday's excitement was already a thing of the past. A few hours had been given up to watching distant puffs of cannon-smoke, an evening devoted to noisy celebrations, with singing crowds and candles burning in every window throughout the city. Now it was finished. The French had fallen back to their base on the coast, their attempt abandoned. There seemed no reason why lessons should not start again.

Mark thought otherwise.

A great restlessness seized him as he opened his Latin book. Who wanted to read about the Gauls capturing Rome in 390 B.C. when he had just seen them, with his own eyes, fail to do so in A.D. 1849? Rebellion stirred within him, as it had stirred on that day when he had first realised that, by hook or by crook, he must break away from his grandmother's domination.

With this feeling came the bitter knowledge that he had missed a chance.

Why couldn't he have been with Pietro yesterday? He could have aimed a musket just as straight, he was sure. The idea had never struck him at the time. If it had, he would have dismissed it as impossible. Now, too late, he saw that it wouldn't have been. Boys of sixteen, fifteen, even fourteen, had been in the battle. Being a foreigner had made no difference. English, Belgian and Dutch artists had fought in the ranks. Even a Frenchman, disgusted with his own government. Nor had Bilibin, as it happened, presented any problem. Since Mark *had* been able to slip away on his own, he might just as well have been with Pietro in the Pamfili gardens instead of with Tessa watching from the walls.

'You are very inattentive this afternoon,' Bilibin complained. 'I fear that you overtired yourself yesterday. We must remember how delicate you are. The weather is getting extremely hot.'

'I'm all right, sir.'

Mark tried to fix his mind on the page of Livy in front of him, but his thoughts kept ranging wildly away.

When they met MacWhirter at the café that evening, the Palmas were already sitting with him. The artist explained that Pietro had been giving him some first-hand details to include in the dispatch he was sending to his editor.

'Though my impressions were so confused,' laughed Pietro modestly, 'that I think Mr. MacWhirter knows more about it than I do. I just fired my gun and ran with the others.'

'Do not talk nonsense,' said Tessa, aglow with pride.

Pietro was still in uniform, which did not improve Mark's temper. Nor did the waiter's respectful manner.

'How long are you going to wear this get-up?' Mark asked. 'It doesn't fit. Of course, it must be a great help getting waiters to serve you quickly.'

'Yes, isn't it dreadful?' Pietro beamed — he was incapable of taking offence. Tessa was less pleased.

'He will wear his uniform as long as it is necessary. Do you imagine the danger is all over?'

'You mean — the French may come back?'

'They may. Meanwhile the Spaniards may try something, there are the Austrians in the north — and Bomba is camped not twenty miles away.'

By this time Mark did not need to ask who 'Bomba' was. He knew it was the nickname bestowed on King Ferdinand of Naples after the murderous bombardment of his own subjects in Catania and Messina when Sicily revolted against him.

MacWhirter seemed to sense the awkward atmosphere. He broke in so that the conversation could become more general. 'It's lucky,' he said, 'that Bomba and the French are as jealous of each other as a couple of cats. If they'd worked together, they could have cracked Rome open like a nut — Bomba could have come up from the east as Oudinot made his attack from the west. But Bomba wants all the glory for himself.'

The King of Naples seemed in no immediate hurry to seek this glory. He was encamped with ten thousand men at the foot of the Alban Hills, almost within sight. So long as he remained there he was a constant menace to the city. Because of him, Mazzini had forbidden Garibaldi to go after the French in the opposite direction.

'Rome must not be left defenceless,' said Pietro with the gravity of an old soldier. 'Rome needs every man she has — and more.'

Tessa nodded vigorously. Her eyes rested fondly on

96

her brother's uniform. Mark caught her look, and felt more restless than ever.

Rome had a cheerful, almost festive atmosphere for the next few days. The French made no move to re-open hostilities. Perhaps it had all been a dreadful mistake, perhaps the French Government had misunderstood the whole situation in Rome and would now agree to a friendly settlement, realising that the Pope was perfectly free to return to the city if he so wished? The French prisoners were treated more like guests than enemies and taken on sightseeing trips, while their wounded were nursed in the emergency hospitals opened in some of the churches. When they were fit enough to travel, all were set free. In return, General Oudinot released the captured friar and a company of four hundred volunteers from Bologna, whom, like the Lombards earlier, he had intercepted on their way to Rome.

So, bit by bit, life returned to normal. Mark wrestled with Latin and Greek, traipsed sulkily round ruins, carried round tea-cups to Miss Ellis and other ladies at an English tea-party, and saw the Palmas whenever Pietro's duties and his own allowed. This he began to enjoy again as his jealousy faded. Pietro was such a good sort, Tessa so lively and warm-hearted, it was impossible not to like both of them.

He was suggesting an arrangement for the following day when an embarrassed expression came into Pietro's face.

'Not tomorrow. I am sorry, I cannot.'

'The next day, then?'

'I am so sorry, Marco. That also is impossible.'

Mark stared. 'When *can* we meet then?'

'It — it is very difficult for me to say. To make any arrangements for the future. Just now.'

'I see.'

The silence was awkward. Mark did not know what to say. Pietro seemed to be struggling inwardly. Suddenly he blurted out:

'I am not supposed to say — but perhaps it does not count telling you, a foreigner and a friend. But you must swear to tell no one else, not even Mr. Bilibin or Mr. MacWhirter.'

'I swear.'

Pietro lowered his voice. 'We are ordered on an expedition. With Garibaldi. I think — I do not know — that we are going to make a raid on the Neapolitans. We parade tomorrow evening. Now you understand why I cannot make any arrangements? I do not know how many days we shall be gone.' Pietro fixed his mild eyes on Mark anxiously. 'I can trust you? Not a word of this to anyone?'

'I've sworn, haven't I?' Mark swallowed and took the plunge. 'And now, Pietro, it's your turn. You've got to swear that *you* won't tell Bilibin either . . .'

He began to unfold his plan.

It was almost unbelievably easy.

Neither Pietro nor Tessa argued about it: to them it was just splendid and the most natural thing in the world. Enrolling in the Student Corps was equally simple. There were no formalities, no awkward questions, almost nothing in fact beyond a warm handshake and the issue of a blue tunic, a musket, and a few other items of equipment, which the Palmas promised to look after until the evening. The hardest part was the note to Bilibin, telling him not to worry. Mark was sure he would be back, safe and sound, within a few days. *'There is no need to write home and upset my grandmother . . .'*

Pietro's new comrades of the Student Corps received the latest recruit with casual friendliness. There was no complicated drill to learn. The few Italian words of command were obvious and nobody seemed to mind if you turned right instead of left or were a split second slower than your neighbours. The men formed up in their ranks much as they pleased, not according to height but by friendship. Mark found he was to march in a four including Pietro, an art student from Brussels, named Jacques something, and a young Roman journalist, Lorenzo Bellotti.

He felt terribly nervous as they waited on the parade-ground in the gathering dusk. The preliminaries seemed endless — the long whispered discussions between the officers, the slow doling out of ammunition, the comings and goings of messengers, the false alarms that they were about to move off. Would they *never* start? He had a nightmare vision of Bilibin making a sudden appearance, clutching the farewell letter in one hand and a Union Jack in the other, scouring the ranks to discover his truant pupil and lead him away by the ear.

It was all so free and easy, so amateurish. Garibaldi moved about, a cigar between his teeth, exchanging a few words here and there with officers and men alike. There were no smart salutes, no rigid standing to attention. The Belgian artist laughed at Mark's surprise and said in French:

'It's only on the battlefield that the General demands discipline. He does not mind at other times.'

The Lombard volunteers made a striking contrast with the rest of the parade. They were lined up at one side, standing at ease, but orderly to the rolling of the last cape and the adjustment of the last knapsack. To-night they were released from the parole they had given to the French. Tomorrow, the fifth of May, they would be free to fight for Italy again.

Mark had picked up MacWhirter's journalistic trick of registering details and estimating numbers. He judged that there must be well over two thousand men mustering there in the twilight — half of them Garibaldi's own Legion, the rest students, other volunteers, the Lombard Bersaglieri, and a handful of dragoons. MacWhirter would be grateful for *his* impressions when he got back . . .

It was quite dark when they moved off.

'Garibaldi's a great one for night marches,' Jacques explained. 'He likes to keep the enemy guessing — they never know where he'll appear.'

'Lucky for me,' Mark muttered to Pietro. 'If we'd started in daylight I'd never have given Bilibin the slip. By tomorrow it'll be too late for him to do anything.'

They had expected to march out by one of the south-easterly gates which faced across the plain towards the Alban Hills. But Garibaldi never did the obvious thing. He led them out through the Porta San Lorenzo and then along a road which the young Roman, Bellotti, identified with a chuckle as the way to Tivoli. Pietro interpreted to Mark:

'He says the fox is up to his usual tricks. Even when Bomba hears we're on the move, he'll think we're heading in another direction.'

Conversation slackened after the first two or three miles and then almost died away. The countryside slept. There were their own monotonous footfalls and the occasional clop of hoofs and jingle of harness as an officer moved up and down the column. Nothing else but the lovely liquid chirring of nightingales all round them in the scented gloom . . . Over the black blur of the pines rode the young moon, thin and sharp as a reaping-hook.

Once Pietro whispered: 'You are not tired?'

'No.'

So far this steady tramp across the plain was nothing. Mark had often walked for miles along the razor-back skyline of the Malverns, scrambled up slopes like house-roofs, picked his difficult way through woodland and spinney — even Grandmother's cotton-wool programme had allowed for country walks. And (though this would have been news to Mrs. Apperley) the weight of a gun on his shoulder was not an entirely new experience. There had been a friendly gamekeeper who, like the groom Owen, had been concerned lest he should grow up soft and unmanly. Grandmother could not have eyes on every acre of Worcestershire at once.

Tonight there was a fever of excitement in his blood which made him unconscious of the miles and gave everything an unreal dream-like quality. He was another person. No longer Mark Apperley, the frustrated boy, chivvied, cosseted, corrected — above all, captive. He was free. A man now.

Words whirled in his head, formed and re-formed themselves into sentences. He imagined himself a special correspondent like MacWhirter, scribbling dispatches while the bullets flew. Quite often, in the last few days, he had envied MacWhirter his profession, wished he had the same artistic gifts. Never mind, whatever Mac-Whirter said, the newspapers would always need words as well as pictures. As he tramped doggedly forward he saw before his eyes not the vague heads and shoulders of the young men in front but a printed page, bold in its black and white.

'From Our Special Correspondent with General Garibaldi's Forces

'Tonight I am accompanying General Garibaldi's column of some 2,200 men, which quitted Rome secretly after dark for an unknown destination. It is widely supposed that the objective is a surprise attack on the army of Naples, but that Garibaldi, being outnumbered four to one by the King's forces, is resorting to the same guerrilla tactics which he first developed in South America and has more recently employed to such advantage against the Austrians in Northern Italy . . . '

Yes, it would have looked well in a newspaper. Perhaps someday——

The column marched on. The earth turned, the star-pattern overhead changed, the sickle-moon went down, pale dawn began to outline the Sabine Hills in front. Suddenly Mark realised that he had a blistered heel, that his legs ached, and that the musket lay like an iron girder on his shoulder.

In the morning they made camp amid the straggling ruins of Hadrian's Villa. Mark smiled when he learnt where the fifteen-mile march had brought them. Bilibin had been planning an excursion to this very spot in a hired carriage laden with picnic-basket, Miss Ellis, and everything essential for an enjoyable day out. Bilibin would have led them round the one-time emperor's retreat, identifying each heap of rubble and silencing even the cicadas with his flow of historical references.

How differently the visit had turned out! Smoke curled from a hundred fires, piled muskets stood about in slanting stacks, hobbled horses munched the grass, red-shirted veterans of the pampas opened their strange saddles and unrolled them to create, like magic, little bivouac tents. Others rode off, swinging their lassoes, and returned driving sheep and cattle which they proceeded to slaughter in a matter-of-fact manner.

'Ugh!' Pietro shuddered and turned away. 'I saw plenty of blood that day at the Pamfili, but this is different.'

'I've seen pigs killed at home,' said Mark, 'though I wasn't supposed to. Pigs are worse.'

Even Pietro recovered his appetite when the smell of cooking began to mingle with the tang of wood-smoke and he was ready to tackle his slice of beef without grumbling at its toughness.

Some of the students, however, began to complain that there was no wine. Then, suddenly, the noisy voices were all hushed together. Looking round to find the reason, Mark saw Garibaldi standing silently behind him, his eyes sombre with anger. He waited, letting his disapproval sink in. Then he said, and even Mark caught his meaning:

'Must you call for wine already? You have been going only a few hours. For five years I made do with water in South America.'

He turned and stalked away. After that they all filled their drinking-mugs at a stream, Mark with the others, heedless of his grandmother's forebodings. Then at last, blessed moment, they were really free to take off their boots, make pillows of their knapsacks, and fling themselves down to sleep in the shadow of the orange-groves.

'*Palestrina, May 9th.*' Once more 'Our Special Correspondent' in his own imagination, Mark whiled away a dull hour of guard-duty by composing dispatches for his non-existent newspaper.

'*I am now in a position to disclose . . .* '

A good phrase. All the best journalists used it. Mac-Whirter had said so. It implied that you had known the facts all along, even when in fact you had only just been told them.

'*I am now in a position to disclose General Garibaldi's design, which hitherto I could not reveal owing to the exigencies of the military situation.*'

Another good phrase. But it was as well that he did not need to spell 'exigencies'.

'We marched here two days ago from Hadrian's Villa. Palestrina is an ancient walled town, fifteen hundred feet up, looking across a wide plain towards the Alban Hills where the Neapolitan army lies. It is thus an ideal base for raiding their lines of communication and preventing their further advance upon Rome. Several successful skirmishes have already inflicted losses upon them.'

Here Mark's inspiration deserted him. The Student Corps had not been allowed to join in these guerrilla raids. He was already tired of the sleepy little town. There was nothing to do but wander up and down its steep cobbled lanes — some of them more like staircases than streets — eat two unattractive meals a day, clean the musket he had never fired, and (as now) do an hour's duty at the Rome Gate watching the occasional donkey or bullock-cart pass by.

Pietro appeared at his elbow, peering wistfully towards the city which they could see, ever so faintly, in the heat-haze of noon.

'I hope Tessa is all right.'

'Sure to be. Trust *her*!'

Pietro sighed. 'I wish something would happen.'

'So do I.'

'No, I do not mean just now, today. The whole situation. I do not want to spend all my life doing this. I am not a soldier. I am — I want to be — an engineer.' There in the quiet shadow of the gateway Pietro talked of his plans more earnestly than Mark had ever heard him talk before. 'When all this is over, and when the Austrians are cleared out of the North also, we shall go to Verona. At least, I shall take Tessa to Verona, for that is our old home. An engineer must live where the work is. I must make money and save. It will not be easy, but it is necessary, or Tessa cannot marry.'

'Why ever not?'

'In this country a respectable girl cannot marry without a dowry. Girls marry young. Tessa is little more than a child, I know, but in three or four years she will be — what did they call it in London? — "on the shelf". So, as Papa is dead, I have this responsibility. I must become an engineer, I must save money, I must see that Tessa is happily married to some good young man in Verona. Only then can I think about a nice girl for myself. And before I can even commence this programme,' he added with a wry laugh, 'I have to free my country. With, of course, a little assistance from General Garibaldi and the gallant English adventurer, Marco Apperley!'

'H'm, it *is* rather a programme. I don't wonder you're impatient to get on with it.'

'Marco! Look—— '

Pietro's tone had changed. He pointed. Something was moving in the plain below, a long dust-cloud like a woolly grey caterpillar inching itself along the road. A mile to the left, on the parallel road which entered Palestrina by the Valmontone Gate, there was another advancing column.

Mark let out a gasp of horror. 'I shouldn't have been talking—— ' he stammered guiltily.

'Don't worry. Shout for the sergeant.' Pietro faded tactfully into the background while Mark raised the alarm, making up for his previous slackness by the loudness of his yell. Not only the sergeant but the whole guard came running out of the gatehouse, muskets at the ready.

As it happened, Mark need not have been so appalled. Garibaldi was too old a soldier to rely on a single sentry. The Neapolitans had been sighted a quarter of an hour earlier by watchers on the Castel San Pietro, a thousand feet above the town. Even as the students sprang to arms at the Rome Gate the whole of Palestrina awoke behind them from the noonday drowsiness into which it had just sunk. Bugles rang out, drums beat, and the inhabitants, not to be outdone, started to ring their bells. Immediately, with loud lamentations and appeals to the saints, fugitives began to stream in from the scattered houses which stood outside the protection of the walls.

Mark and his companions stood ready to bar the ancient gates as soon as the last of these people were safely inside. But it seemed that there was to be no siege. Garibaldi always preferred to do the attacking himself, and now the Legion came clattering down the cobbled street at the double, eager to come to grips with their enemies in the open.

'We're to stay here in reserve — for the moment,' Pietro interpreted the sergeant's shouted orders. 'Come on up the stairs. We're to line the battlements so we can fire down if we get the chance. But not till we get the word!'

From their lofty position on the top of the gatehouse they had a splendid view of what was happening. The Neapolitan column was now winding up the last few hundred yards of the steep mountain road. The men looked magnificent in their towering shakoes, long-tailed tunics splendid with epaulettes and pipe-clayed cross-belts, and immaculate pantaloons.

'The uniforms of Naples are always superb,' said Jacques with a sneer. 'However, it is the men inside them who count.'

To Mark the enemy seemed formidable enough. There were far too many of them for his liking. In the rear he could see a mass of cavalry. Luckily this place — even the open ground in front of the gates — was not good for horsemen. It was too much broken up with vine-yard walls and hedges, with precipitous slopes and gulleys.

There was an outbreak of firing in the distance.

'That's Colonel Manara and his Lombards,' muttered Pietro. 'They're holding the Valmontone Gate.'

The Legion was now deployed along the base of the wall below them. A bugle sounded the charge and for the first time Mark saw, with almost unbearable excite-ment, the forward rush of Garibaldi's volunteers. The drab scarecrow figures, with only here and there a bright red shirt, made an odd contrast with the elegant array blocking the road in front of them.

'Like street-urchins,' Jacques commented afterwards, 'attacking the chorus of an opera!'

At the time, though, it was no laughing matter. The Neapolitans levelled their muskets with parade-ground precision and fired. Dirty smoke bellied out along the line, some of the racing scarecrows staggered and drop-ped, a few wild shots went so high that they chipped the battlements or even whined over the students' heads, making them duck instinctively . . . Peering over again with more caution, Mark saw that the charge of the Legion had been halted. The Neapolitan fire was altogether too hot. While the front ranks of the enemy column held their ground in the roadway, others had slipped inside the abandoned houses to right and left. Now, from the cover of shuttered windows, they were sniping at the unprotected legionaries.

Had the General blundered? It was the Neapolitans who now had the advantage of fighting from behind thick walls. As the legionaries sullenly dropped back, kneeling to shoot, helping their wounded to limp along, Mark had his doubts. A distant roar of cheering caused the students to exchange questioning glances. What had happened at the Valmontone Gate? Had the other Neapolitan column broken into the town?

That fear at least was soon removed. A passing runner called up the glad news he was taking to Garibaldi: Colonel Manara had launched a similar charge against the troops facing him, the Neapolitans had broken after a few minutes, and they were now in utter rout. Colonel Manara could spare a company of Bersaglieri if the General needed reinforcements.

Half an hour later they saw the jaunty cock's feathers of the victorious Lombards bobbing in the street behind the gate-house, ready to help when the next attack was mounted.

'We can do with them,' said Pietro grimly. 'We'll need every man, I should think.'

'Manifestly,' said Jacques, 'it is the main force of the enemy that we have to deal with here.'

The sergeant shouted something. They turned and began to file down the stone stairway. Pietro touched Mark's sleeve.

'We too——' he whispered.

Mark swallowed but said nothing.

The streets and alleys just inside the gate were solid with men. The hot afternoon air reeked with sweat and gunpowder. High above the slanting bayonets Garibaldi sat his horse, granite-faced, gently edging his way forward through the ranks. His white *poncho* vanished into the shadows of the archway. Aguyar and a handful of other riders filed after him. There was cheering outside. The enemy's fire grew hotter.

'It's worse,' Mark muttered, 'waiting — when you can't see anything.'

'Yes.'

Had the ancient gladiators felt like this as they waited for their cue outside the arena? Mark smiled to himself. That was the sort of thing which would have occurred to old Bilibin at a moment like this.

A bugle sounded. A queer, blood-curdling noise these bugles made, a sort of bray, shrill, rather unpleasant . . .

'*Avanti!*'

But that was for the Bersaglieri. They doubled through the archway in neat column of fours, their fine rifles all held up at the same angle, their bayonets aligned as perfectly as the spikes on a railing.

Then came the awaited order: '*Studenti! Avanti!*'

Dry mouthed, Mark plunged forward with the rest, into the echoing gloom of the archway, out into the blinding glare of the sun.

Here there was a momentary check. Officers with out-flung arms marshalled them into line. The Lombards had gone on, fanning out across the littered ground. Mark saw them going forward shoulder to shoulder with the legionaries. Garibaldi on his white horse, pointing with his sabre, was outlined against the battle-smoke. A fierce hand-to-hand struggle was raging. The firing slackened, the smoke thinned and skeined away. Now it was all lurching heads and thrusting bayonets.

Again the cry: '*Avanti!*' The students raced forward with a yell. Down the stony road, slithering, stumbling, swerving to avoid a body, jumping over ditches ... And, as they went, the shuttered windows and barricaded balconies began to spit flame again. Bullets screeched as they grooved stone walls. Splinters flew. Mark felt a searing cut across his knuckles and saw that his uplifted left hand was red with blood.

The mêlée in front had suddenly dissolved into hundreds of separate figures. The Neapolitans had broken before the onset of Legion and Bersaglieri combined. They were in panic-stricken flight down the zigzag road. Some of the volunteers rushed after them, others paused to shoot, others turned their attention to the enemy in the houses.

At this critical moment the Neapolitan general threw in his cavalry.

They came thundering up the hill, a tide of tossing plumes and cruelly-flashing sabres, an irresistible weight of hurtling horse-flesh tipped with steel. There were hundreds and hundreds of them. Sickly, Mark realised that there were only a few dozen dragoons to pit against them.

The Student Corps halted in their path. Their commander shouted an instruction. Up went the muskets all along the line.

'He says shoot at the horses,' Pietro panted. 'If we aim at the men we'll miss entirely!'

Mark knew it was sound advice but he could not bring himself to follow it. When his musket went off with the others he never knew whether the bullet had sailed harmlessly over all those shining helmets or whether it had caused one of the empty saddles which now shattered the proud pattern of the squadron in front of him.

The fighting became fluid. The horsemen came on in clusters, in ones and twos. The impetus was gone. They wheeled slowly, poking and hacking at the men who dodged around them, poking back with their bayonets. Some of the legionaries leapt in murderously with their daggers. The Lombards fired their rifles calmly and with accuracy. One rider after another toppled from his horse. The Neapolitans were not men to fight to the death. Soon they were all galloping down the mountain-side again.

'Are you all right?' said Pietro anxiously.

'All right?' Mark tried to shake himself back into normality.

'Your hand — there's blood—— '

'Only a graze.'

'I was afraid that man's sword—— '

'What man?'

Pietro laughed. 'The one you were trying to pull off his horse. You were like a madman.'

'I don't really remember — it was all a wild muddle.'

A bullet whined overhead. There was a rumble of hoofs, they swung round and raised their bayonet-points, but it was no hostile trooper. Garibaldi reined in, shouted a terse phrase, and pointed with his sabre at a near-by house from which the Neapolitans were still firing.

'Come on!' cried Pietro.

They pelted across the sunbaked ground. Other students and some of the legionaries were already converging upon the building. Every few seconds there was a flash from one of the shuttered windows. The boys ducked and scrambled through some vines, crossed a yard under cover of a cart, and made a dash for the house, flattening themselves against the blank wall where they were safe from the men inside. Then, having recovered their breath, they slid round the angle of the building to where Jacques and Bellotti were battering at some shutters.

'You want to prise 'em open with the bayonet!' Mark yelled.

'Good idea!' Pietro answered. He straightened up and slipped the thin blade between the shutter and the wall, using his musket as a lever to break away the hinge. As he struggled, there was a deafening bang and a spurt of flame from a loophole just above his head. Mark saw his friend drop to his knees and his hat go flying. In that instant he saw himself — in fancy, this time — breaking the news of Pietro's death to Tessa. Then, to his relief, Pietro jumped to his feet again. Meanwhile, half a dozen legionaries had found a log and were pounding the door. It yielded. They rushed in with blood-freezing howls. The students followed, scrambling over benches and mattresses which had been piled up as a barricade. A wounded Neapolitan met them on his knees, pleading for mercy. Two more, their empty hands uplifted, emerged from the next room, shepherded by a legionary. Shouts, shots, and racing footsteps indicated that their companions were making a belated attempt to escape by another doorway.

Pietro went out to find his hat. There was a scorch-mark across the brim. His glossy hair was singed above his left ear.

'It will take more than that to kill me,' he boasted happily.

Resistance was now over. A pathetic file of King Bomba's warriors was wending its way through the Rome Gate under escort. The wounded and dead were being cleared from the scene. But the vast majority of the five thousand men who had marched against Palestrina were miles away, some in organized retreat, many in headlong rout.

That evening there were wild rejoicings in the little town. The wine flowed, lights burned golden at every window, the mountain echoed with the strains of *Fratelli d'Italia*. The students talked cheerfully of marching on against Bomba himself and chasing him, with his whole army of tailor's dummies, right back to Naples.

The next day brought more sober thoughts. There was news from Rome. Nobody knew anything for certain, but the rumour ran round that the French were about to attack the city again and that Mazzini had ordered Garibaldi back. The General, as usual, kept his own counsel:

his moves were always kept secret till the last possible minute. But nobody was surprised when the word came to parade in marching order at sunset — or when the column left by way of the Rome Gate and headed westwards for the city which they had left only a week before.

Chapter Eight

WORDS OF HONOUR

BILIBIN was at breakfast. He leapt to his feet and flung out his arms, stammering.

'M-Mark, my b-boy! Are you all right?'

'Bit tired, sir.' Mark slipped off his knapsack and fell, rather than sat down, on the sofa. 'That coffee smells good — do you think, sir, I might——'

'Of course!' Bilibin rang the bell. 'You look dead beat. I shall send for a doctor——'

'I'm all *right*, sir. I just want some sleep.'

'What on earth have they done to you?'

'Just one of the General's famous night-marches.' Mark tried to smile reassuringly and achieved a ghastly grin. 'We've been on the road since dusk yesterday. It's twenty miles from Palestrina. And we had to dodge Bomba's main army.'

'You were at Palestrina when the battle was fought?'

'I was *in* the battle.'

Bilibin groaned. 'This is a nightmare. What shall we tell Mrs. Apperley? I began a letter last night — I dared not delay any longer — I was going to post it this morning. I did not know *what* to say . . .'

'Need you say anything now, sir? Why not tear it up?'

Fresh coffee arrived. Mark dragged himself to the table

and began to wolf down rolls and butter. There were heavy footsteps on the stairs and the door was flung open.

'Garibaldi's back! Now you should have news——' MacWhirter stopped. His sandy eyebrows shot up and his face became a sunrise. 'Ah! So the prodigal's returned already! I'll have something to say to you, laddie. Running off like that, driving Mr. Bilibin nearly out of his wits with worry!'

'I shall have plenty to say to him myself.' Bilibin spoke with a severity which would have scared Mark if he had not been too tired to feel any emotion. 'Leave him alone, now, MacWhirter. He must go straight to bed. Do you realise he has marched all the way from Palestrina?'

'He has? Splendid!' MacWhirter pulled up a chair beside Mark, whipped out his note-book, and licked his pencil. 'Then he can just answer a few questions.'

'MacWhirter! Not now. The boy's exhausted. Questions must wait.'

'The post won't. I'm not going to hold back my dispatch for a whole day while he sleeps the clock round!'

'It's inhuman——'

'It's journalism.'

'I can't permit it.'

'My dear Bilibin, you can't stop it.'

'Please, sir,' begged Mark wearily, 'it will be simpler if I just tell Mr. MacWhirter what he wants to know.'

'It always is,' said the Scotsman cheerfully. 'Look, laddie, if you've finished your breakfast, why not talk to me while you undress? Then you can tumble straight into bed and we'll not disturb you any more.'

'If you like, sir.'

They all went up to Mark's room. Wearily he peeled off his shoddy uniform and washed off the dust of the road, talking all the time. MacWhirter interrupted only to prompt and question, Bilibin only to exclaim in horror at the state of his feet and to insist on fetching ointment and bandages. At last came the sweet moment Mark had often dreamed of during the weary night hours, when he slid his aching body between the cool linen sheets and laid his cheek on a pillow that was unbelievably soft.

He was dimly conscious that Bilibin was closing the shutters against the morning glare and that the two men were whispering as they tiptoed out. From a great distance came MacWhirter's husky voice.

'I'll allow, Bilibin, he's a tiresome devil, but I'll tell you this — he's a born journalist!'

And the clergyman's tart reply: 'I have noticed that the two things often go together.'

MacWhirter chuckled, the door closed softly, and Mark was aware of nothing more until the evening.

It was seven o'clock when he woke up, ravenous. The clamour of a Roman evening rose from the street and came throbbing into the dark room. When he flung back the shutters it was like the roar of an opened furnace.

His uniform had vanished, tidied away no doubt. He put on clean clothes. Never in his life before had he realised what exquisite pleasure could spring from pulling down a crisp fresh shirt over one's shoulders and slip-

ping one's feet into cool shoes which someone else had
polished to a glossy perfection.

He went down to the sitting-room. Bilibin laid aside
the book he was reading. Mark looked round anxiously.
He remembered propping his musket in the corner of
the room when he first staggered in, but it was there no
longer. He felt ashamed of forgetting the rule impressed
upon him in the Student Corps, never to be parted from
his weapon.

Bilibin knew what he was looking for. 'Your gun,'
he remarked with grim satisfaction, 'has been returned
to the appropriate authorities. With the rest of the
equipment.'

'*Returned*, sir?' Mark gaped.

'Of course.'

'But—— '

'You surely did not think that this absurd charade
could be permitted to continue?'

Mark said, in a low voice: 'It was not a charade, sir.'
If Bilibin heard, he took no notice.

'I have been frantic this past week, frantic! I went to
the British Consul, I went to the Ministry of War — nobody could do anything to help me—— '

'I'm sorry, sir. I did say in my note—— '

'That you had gone with Garibaldi! But nobody knew
where Garibaldi was. Or, if they did, nobody would
say. You had vanished. There was no means of getting
into touch with you. You had put me in an impossible
position. I was responsible for your safety. If anything
had happened to you——' Bilibin almost choked with
emotion.

Mark saw his point. 'I do apologize, sir.'

'Apologies are not enough. I also want your word of honour that you will not go rushing off with Pietro like this again.'

Mark licked his lips. 'I — I'm not sure that I can promise that, sir.'

'Are you defying me?'

'Oh, no, sir! I do see that it's terribly difficult for you, sir,' said Mark earnestly, 'but if we're going to talk of "honour" it's not very easy for me. I joined the Student Corps. I can't be treated like a child now.'

'You *are* a child. In law. Even if you had run off to join the British Army you would have had to come out again. You are too young.'

'It's different here, sir——'

'I am well aware of that! But even these wild Italians have some regard for what is proper. You are a British subject. Mr. Mazzini will not wish to annoy Her Majesty's Government just to keep one boy in the ranks against the express wishes of his lawful guardian.'

Mark glowered at his tutor. Bilibin had a point there. He felt the ground slipping from under his feet. It was infuriating, after tasting independence, after living a man's life for the past week, to find himself helpless again.

There was a tap on the door. 'Come in,' said Bilibin irritably. He looked even more irritated when the door opened to reveal Pietro and Tessa. Pietro was in uniform, which his sister had obviously sponged and pressed. He bowed.

'Good evening, Mr. Bilibin. We called to inquire if Marco is all right——'

'I am very glad to see you,' said Bilibin grimly. 'Kindly shut the door.'

They accepted the chairs he offered them. Tessa gave Mark a look which consoled him for the unpleasantness of the last few minutes.

'I will not beat about the bush, young man. I have just asked Mark for his word of honour that he will not run off with you again. I must now ask you to give me a similar assurance.'

Pietro hesitated. He turned troubled eyes on Mark. It was Tessa who broke into the awkward silence.

'Mr. Bilibin! Why should not Mark go with my brother again if he wishes to?'

'Because he is too young.'

'He was not too young to fight at Palestrina! There are other boys as young!'

'That may be so. If their parents permit them to go and get killed, that is their business. But Mark is English. All this fighting is no affair of his——'

'That is not so!' Tessa interrupted him excitedly. 'Is not freedom everybody's affair? And especially the affair of you English?'

'Tessa!' her brother protested weakly.

'Let Mr. Bilibin answer. Is not that what the newspapers were always saying when we lived in London?'

Even Bilibin's new firmness wilted somewhat before her attack. 'That is as may be. But I am not to be drawn into a political discussion. You too are very young, and a lady, and neither is a good qualification for understanding these matters, if you will forgive my saying so.'

'I will not forgive you!'

'*Tessa!*'

'But, Pietro, how can he say I do not understand these things? When Papa taught us from our earliest years——'

'Mr. Bilibin is talking to me, Tessa. Or trying to! You will forgive my sister, sir? She gets excited,' said Pietro unnecessarily. 'I admit that I am largely responsible for what Marco did.'

'No——' interjected Mark, but his friend went on, ignoring him.

'You demand my assurance that I will not encourage him to do the same again?'

'I most certainly do.'

'And if I do not give you that assurance?'

'In that case,' said Bilibin stiffly, 'I shall be reluctantly compelled to regard you and your sister as unsuitable friends for Mark. And I mean reluctantly,' he added with obvious sincerity, 'for I have nothing else against you and I was only too happy for Mark to have companionship of his own age. But my first duty is to Mrs. Apperley, who has put me in a position of trust——'

'I understand that, sir.'

'So, painful though it would be, I should have no alternative. I should have to forbid Mark to see or communicate with either of you. And I should request you, as a matter of courtesy, to respect my wishes and not ask him to disobey me.'

There was a heavy silence. Even Tessa was subdued.

'Further,' said Bilibin, 'I should have to take the first opportunity of removing Mark from Rome.'

'All right, sir,' said Mark gloomily. 'You've got us in a cleft stick.'

'You won't go off with Pietro again?'

'No, sir.'

'And I give you my word, sir,' said Pietro earnestly, 'I will do nothing against your wishes.'

'And as *I* am "very young" and "a lady" as well, my opinion is too unimportant to matter,' said Tessa. Bilibin, having won, made no comment but gave her a smile of sweet forgiveness. It was not returned.

Pietro took her away rather hurriedly. The signs were not promising for a happy evening all together.

MacWhirter came in later and insisted on taking them out to a café for a little while. He was very grateful to Mark for giving him such an accurate eye-witness account of the Palestrina expedition, but he had to conceal this for fear of annoying Bilibin. He took the first opportunity to whisper to Mark:

'Old Bilibin's still a bit ruffled — you must make allowances — you've given him a frightful time, you know——'

'I realise that, and I'm sorry, sir.'

'Don't worry too much. He's had compensations.'

'Compensations?'

'Miss Ellis was most sympathetic. When he was running round all distracted, she did her best to comfort him — she was much more successful than I was.'

'She's nice.'

'She doesn't think *you're* nice,' MacWhirter warned him with a chuckle. 'She told me you were a Perpetual Problem. And so you are, of course.'

The next few days did a little to ease the smart of Mark's humiliation.

It was a false alarm which had brought them back to Rome. Though the French had built up their forces strongly and had moved closer to the city, they made no attack, and Mark did not have to stand idly by (as he had feared) while his late comrades defended the ramparts. There were, indeed, high hopes of peace. A Monsieur de Lesseps had arrived from Paris to discuss an armistice. Pietro and the others were just kicking their heels, and Mark (though he could not stroll about in uniform) had the satisfaction of knowing that he was just as much one of the victorious veterans of Palestrina. And Tessa treated him accordingly.

She had found work, now, to eke out her brother's scanty pay. She went for several hours to look after the children of an English lady, an author's wife, who lived near the Spanish Steps. MacWhirter had recommended her and the lady had jumped at the chance of a nurse-maid who had grown up in London.

'She says I am not like an Italian girl at all,' Tessa reported furiously. 'She thinks she is paying me a compliment!'

However, the children were 'pets', the money was welcome, and she was spared the loneliness when Pietro was on duty. And when Pietro ran in to tell Mark that he was under orders to leave Rome again, he was able to add that Tessa was moving into the English lady's house while he was away.

'Where are you going this time? Or is it secret?' Mark asked wistfully. All his restlessness had come back with a rush. But they had both given their word to Bilibin. The situation had to be accepted.

'No secret this time.' Pietro laughed. 'You can't move ten thousand men without the news getting round.'

'Ten thousand!'

'Oh, this is a full-scale affair. Garibaldi's only second-in-command — more's the pity. The Commander-in-Chief is going himself. Roselli. Now we haven't the French to worry about, we can give Bomba our full attention. We're going to chase him back to Naples.' Pietro's eyes were sparkling.

'I wish——' Mark began. But it was no use wishing.

'It is hard lines.' Pietro patted his shoulder. 'Will you keep an eye on Tessa for me?'

'Of course.'

'It is good that she will be staying in this house so close to you. She worries about me — and this time we may be away much longer. If anything happened to me, I know that you . . .' Pietro's voice faltered.

'Don't talk twaddle,' said Mark gruffly. That was the one trouble with these Italians, they so easily got sentimental. Nothing was going to happen to Pietro. He was going on another glorious adventure, lucky dog. That was war, a glorious adventure. Some people would get killed, inevitably, but they would be mostly Neapolitans or unknown strangers anyway. People one knew didn't get killed. At the worst Pietro would come home with his arm in a sling or a bandage round his head, and that would make him doubly a hero.

The day after the troops had marched out against the Neapolitans the armistice with the French became official.

'Mazzini has managed things very well,' MacWhirter

admitted, 'and this de Lesseps seems a reasonable fellow. I'm told they had a flaming row to begin with, but now they're getting on together like a house on fire.'

'Most appropriate!' said Mark.

MacWhirter gave him a sharp look, then gave him a playful punch. 'All right, laddie, all right! When it comes to words, you're the smart one. I'm only an illiterate artist. Well, if you prefer it, de Lesseps and Mazzini get on famously. Which is more than can be said for Garibaldi and his commander-in-chief.'

'Don't *they*, sir?'

MacWhirter shook his tawny head. 'Roselli's a regular soldier, cautious, likes to do everything by the book. And Garibaldi — well, I don't have to tell an old campaigner like you about Garibaldi——'

'Have a heart, sir!' Mark pleaded. MacWhirter's teasing came sometimes a little near the bone.

The Scotsman was right, though, in forecasting trouble between the generals. Roselli's methods maddened his second-in-command. Complaints filtered back to the city, where MacWhirter's shrewd nose for facts soon smelt them out. The food-supply was so badly organized that it was taking all the cattle-rustling skill of Aguyar and other old hands with the lasso to save the troops from hunger. Roselli was moving with such elephantine slowness that Bomba was being given every chance to escape.

Then, one evening, the newspaper-boys came racing down the Corso, yelling news of victory. The Neapolitans had been caught and smashed at Velletri. The territory of the Roman Republic was clear of them.

'Garibaldi did it,' MacWhirter reported to his friends the following day. 'He had to take matters into his own hands and just ignore Roselli, or Bomba's men would have got clean away. Garibaldi took over the advance-guard — which he'd no right to do — sailed in, and gave them a thrashing.' He shook with laughter. 'Roselli was furious. It was a flagrant case of indiscipline on Gari-baldi's part. It was also, incidentally, a decisive victory. Somehow that doesn't entirely console Roselli.'

'There must be respect for authority,' said Bilibin mildly.

'And there's no point in winning a game by breaking the rules, is there? And war *is* just a game with rules, isn't it? Och, man, don't blether!' concluded Mac-Whirter — rather unfairly, since Bilibin had not ventured another word.

As for Mark, his mind was far away across the barren plains of the Campagna, marching forward in triumph shoulder to shoulder with Pietro, Jacques and the rest of them, behind the red-white-and-green flag and the dancing ostrich-plumes of the guerrilla general.

On the last day of the month they watched Garibaldi's victorious return. He looked gaunt and strained, thought Mark. MacWhirter said he was unwell. He was still suffering from the wound he had received during the French attack on the thirtieth of April, and in the fighting at Velletri he and Aguyar had been knocked off their horses, ridden over, and badly trampled. They might have been killed if some young boys in the Legion had not dashed in, heedless of danger, and dragged them clear.

There was nothing strained or unwell about Pietro.
He glanced up at just the right moment, saw his friends
on the balcony, and waved back. His bronzed face was
one huge smile. Jacques and Bellotti were swinging
along at his side. Mark felt a pang as he recognized all
the old faces, and proudly named them for Bilibin and
MacWhirter. Not one face was missing from the
ranks — except his own. No casualties. That was victory
as it should be.

Within an hour or two they were sitting with Pietro
and Tessa in a restaurant, celebrating his safe return.
There was something else to celebrate that evening: de
Lesseps had signed an agreement with Mazzini — and
the terms were so unbelievably good that all Rome was
wild with delight.

France guaranteed to protect Rome and her territory
from all invaders, Austrian, Neapolitan, or otherwise.
General Oudinot would make no attempt to bring his
troops into the city. They would remain in their present
positions outside.

'This is wonderful!' cried Pietro. 'This is better than
we dreamed! Some of us were disappointed because
Mazzini called the army back — we wanted Garibaldi to
lead us on to Naples and knock Bomba off his throne.
But I see now that Mazzini was right. Bomba won't
dare to come here again if the French are protecting
Rome. Garibaldi is free to march north against the
Austrians.' He turned to his sister. 'Do you realise, Tessa?
We're going north! We're going to save Venice, we're
going to liberate our own beautiful Verona, we're going
to kick the *tedeschi* across the Alps where they belong!'

It was a lovely dream. The next morning brought the awakening.

General Oudinot had torn up the agreement. De Lesseps had been recalled to Paris. The French had been using him to gain time while they built up their forces and brought out their heavy siege-artillery.

Oudinot announced that the armistice was over. *'But,'* he wrote to Roselli, *'to give French residents time to leave Rome I shall not attack the place until Monday, the fourth of June.'*

That was on Friday, the first.

Bilibin, to Mark's disgust, immediately started making arrangements to go. They would withdraw to a quiet guest-house at Tivoli, where they could take healthy walks in the Sabine Hills and study Horace's poems in the very district where they had been written. They could also visit Hadrian's Villa, which, he knew, Mark had already seen once — 'but not properly', he added without a trace of a smile.

They were not, however, the only people planning to quit Rome that week-end. Carriages were hard to hire. The earliest departure Bilibin could arrange was on Sunday morning. They would attend Morning Prayer with the other English residents who still remained and then step into their carriage, their bags already loaded, and drive away.

'What can I *do*?' Mark asked Tessa desperately.

She shrugged. Her own employers were not moving. 'You can do nothing,' she said, 'except obey your Mr. Bilibin.'

'*You* don't think I'm funking?'

'No, Marco. There is nothing you can do. Except——'
she smiled. 'You will want to say good-bye to Pietro?'

'Of course!'

'He has been posted to the Pamfili gardens — again!
Will you take me over there tomorrow evening? It is
not so good now for a young girl by herself . . . Pietro
would like it if you escorted me.'

Bilibin raised no objection. He had farewells of his
own to make. And for this last week-end the city was at
peace.

Mark and Tessa made a country walk of it, cutting
across the vine-clad slopes from the gate by St. Peter's.
It was a glorious June evening and a mellow, peach-like
glow lay across the landscape.

Pietro and his friends had made themselves as comfortable as possible in the grounds of the Villa Pamfili.
They were in high spirits. They had driven the French
away before, they could do the same again. They sat
round the small fires on which they were cooking their
supper. One young man produced a guitar and soon a
whole crowd of them were roaring forth patriotic songs
and operatic choruses. Tessa's eyes sparkled as she stood
listening. Mark felt low-spirited, and his spirits were
not raised by the fuss some of the students made of
her.

Suddenly a shout put an end to the singing and they
all leapt to their feet. There on the garden-steps, looking
down on them with a kindly smile, was General Roselli.
He made a brief speech in answer to their cheers. Mark's
knowledge of Italian, joined with his Latin, was enough
now to enable him to catch the rough meaning.

The Commander-in-Chief had come to visit them (he explained) because the gallant General Garibaldi, who was now responsible for the whole western side of the city, was not yet well enough to take up his post. But there was no cause to worry. The French would make no move before Monday — he had General Oudinot's promise of that. By Monday they would have Garibaldi and the full strength of the Legion to help them drive off any attack.

'Meanwhile, sleep well, my boys! It is next week you will want all your energies.'

They broke into cheers again, he saluted and moved away with his staff, and the guitarist struck up *Fratelli d'Italia* once more.

Mark said good-bye to Pietro as casually as he could, dreading an outburst of Italian emotion, but Pietro was so gay that the parting passed off without embarrassment.

'My salutations to Mr. Bilibin!' he called after them. 'Tell him not to forget the fine Roman amphitheatre in Verona. Perhaps we shall all meet there in a month or two, when we have dealt with the Austrians as well!'

'I hope so! I'll tell him.'

Mark escorted Tessa to the house where she was now living. There was no need for them to say good-bye yet. Tessa would be bringing the English children to the service in the morning, having attended Mass herself much earlier.

He went glumly back to his lodgings and, as there seemed nothing to stay up for, obeyed Bilibin's instructions to go to bed early and make sure of a good night's sleep.

He was not destined, however, to enjoy it. It was barely three o'clock when he was awakened by thunder. But *was* it thunder — or distant artillery? He sat bolt upright in the darkness, then leapt out of bed and flung open the shutters. There was no doubt about it. It was gunfire, rolling across the city from the direction of the Villa Pamfili.

Chapter Nine

THE 'ANGLE OF DEATH'

FOR a few moments Mark stood barefoot on the balcony, staring down the empty street. Then he turned back into the room and, without troubling to light a candle, groped for his trousers, socks and shoes. He was half-way down the first flight of stairs when a door opened behind him. There in his night-shirt and night-cap, holding up a candle-stick and gazing blearily over the banisters, was Bilibin.

'Is that you, my boy?'

'Yes, sir!'

'Where in Heaven's name are you going?'

'Only to see what's happening, sir.'

'Mark! Remember what I said! I absolutely forbid you to go rushing off again and——'

'I'm only just going out into the street, sir.' Mark's anxiety made him curt and impatient. 'I must know. I'll be back, I promise.' He fumbled his way down to the next landing. Lights were appearing below, he heard excited voices and the drawing of bolts. . . . He ran down the last flight and slipped between the shadowy, exclaiming figures out into the cool street where, for the time being, he was safe from pursuit.

Other doors were opening, shutters creaking back,

lights making yellow panels on the black wall of the night. As he turned the corner into the Piazza di Spagna a horseman came flying past, sending sparks from the cobbles. He wheeled clattering into the Via della Carozze, where, Mark remembered, Garibaldi had his billet. There, at No. 59, it should be possible to pick up some news. He broke into a run.

There was a cluster of figures round the open door. Officers arrived running in ones and twos, fastening belts and buttons as they pushed their way inside. The light slanted down on faces familiar from the Palestrina expedition. Mark recognized Nino Bixio, the fiery young Genoese, commander of the Legion now that Garibaldi was responsible for the whole western side of the defences, and the twenty-one-year-old poet Mameli, also from Genoa, whom Garibaldi had made his adjutant. He saw Angelo Masina, captain of the lancers from Bologna, hurrying along with the surgeon of the Legion, Ripari. He caught the meaning of a few words Ripari was saying as he passed:

'He insists. He will be all right. A wounded lion is the most dangerous!'

Now, one after another, the tall belfries of the city gave tongue. Bell spoke to bell across the dark rooftops, clanging the alarm, drowning the distant grumble of the guns. Insistently the kettle-drums kept up their ratatatat, calling the troops to arms.

'Laddie! What on earth——'

MacWhirter loomed out of the night. Mark turned to him eagerly. It was a relief to meet someone he could talk to.

'What's happening?' the Scotsman echoed his question. 'That's what *I'm* trying to discover. There's heavy firing across the river. The French must have launched a surprise attack on the Janiculum side.'

'But — sir! They weren't going to do anything before Monday — tomorrow——'

'Well, they have.'

'I heard General Roselli telling the troops so! Only last night. In the Pamfili gardens. Pietro's there.'

'Och, Roselli's a fool! They should have taken no chances. The Pamfili should have been fully manned and ready for anything. They should have fortified the grounds a month ago, straight after that first affair. Garibaldi asked them to. They took no notice. This would never have happened if he'd had his way. And if he hadn't been lying here sick——'

'Look, sir. Aguyar.'

The tall negro came riding up to the door on his black horse. He was leading Garibaldi's well-known white charger. Even as he drew rein, the General came out of the house, a long cigar stuck jauntily between his bearded lips. He moved stiffly, like one in pain. Without a word he climbed into the saddle and was gone. Most of the others followed. MacWhirter managed to button-hole one for a few moments. Then he turned to Mark kindly:

'You'd best get back to bed, laddie. Or to the house, anyhow, to old Bilibin. We'll know more when it's daylight.'

'He said something about the Pamfili—— '

'Ay. The French have got the Pamfili. They blew a

hole in the south boundary-wall, rushed in, and caught the Italians half-asleep.'

'Then — Pietro—— ?'

'Nobody knows anything for certain. A lot of 'em were taken prisoner, a lot escaped and got back to the Villa Corsini. That's where they're fighting now. I don't doubt young Pietro can look after himself. He's a prudent, thoughtful laddie.' MacWhirter patted Mark's shoulder. 'Home with you now. I'll keep my eye open for Pietro — I'll be going up there as soon as it's light enough to see. I'll let you know if I hear anything.'

'Thank you, sir.'

Mark watched him stride away until his burly figure was lost in the gloom. Yes, he must go back to Bilibin. He had promised. But he could not go straight back. He made a slight detour, so as to pass the house where Tessa was staying. There were lights in the upper windows as there were in every other building. No one could sleep in such a din of alarm-bells and gunfire. But the front door was shut, and, though he stood on the opposite side of the street for several wistful minutes, he could not pluck up the courage to ring and ask for Tessa. What could he have said to them? What could he have said to *her*?

Sunday morning dawned. It was strange to be sitting there, drinking coffee and buttering rolls as usual, while from beyond the Janiculum ridge came the growl of guns and the incessant dickering of musketry. Bilibin's round face was sympathetic across the table.

'I know what you must be feeling, dear boy. We should have time, after Morning Prayer, if you like——'

'Have we got to go to church? When people are being killed up there — my friends perhaps — and——'

Bilibin looked shocked, but he kept his tone gentle. 'Perhaps, Mark, it is not such an unsuitable moment for prayer?'

'I'm sorry, sir. I didn't mean——'

'I understand. Listen, Mark. I recall that there is an early service at the English Church this Sunday. Let us go to that.' He nodded towards the open window. 'These Romans are all going to Mass, though it is their city, not ours, that the French are attacking. Then we can walk up to the Porta San Pancrazio and see what is happening. The carriage is not coming until half past twelve.'

'All right, sir. Thank you.'

With that compromise Mark had to be satisfied. It was decent of Bilibin. He too had things on his mind.

The morning was getting really hot by the time they crossed the river and started the stiff climb up the hill. The narrow lane was thronged with hurrying figures. Soldiers, armed civilians, ammunition-carriers, mere spectators like themselves, pushed their way up against a descending stream of stretcher-bearers. A field-hospital had been opened in a near-by church.

'Listen!' Bilibin stopped in his tracks and held up his finger. 'What is that?'

A band was playing from the fortifications above them. Unmistakably, to Mark's horror, it was playing the

Marseillaise. The French must have a footing on the walls by now.

'I think I should take you back,' said Bilibin. 'It is dangerous to go any further if——'

'But, sir, plenty of people are going on in front!'

A passing American stopped to reassure them. 'It's an Italian band. They're playing the *Marseillaise* so that the French can hear them. I hope that dirty dog Oudinot can hear, too. If he's any sense of shame!'

They hurried on up the lane and came out on the wide expanse of waste ground just inside the Porta San Pancrazio. Detachments of the Legion were being reformed there, civilians were being issued with guns and ammunition, Masina was talking to his pathetically tiny group of lancers, dismounted, his left arm in a sling. From the bastion to the right of the gateway the band continued to play, the music oddly sweet and clear against the savage background of the firing. Remembering the words of the *Marseillaise*, Mark wondered if the French would take the hint. They had won *their* freedom in the revolution of sixty years before: why deny it to the Romans now?

'Come on, sir, we can get up on the walls this way——'

'Will they let us?'

'We can try. Tessa and I watched from there before.'

Nobody stopped them. They were not the only sightseers peeping over the sandbagged parapet. Mark half-expected to find Tessa. There was no sign of her. But MacWhirter was there, calmly sharpening his pencil.

'Mind your heads,' he advised. 'There's a few stray bullets fly this way.'

Mark took a cautious look. On the near-by crest stood the Villa Corsini, the 'house of the four winds', magnificent against the cloudless June sky. The slope leading up to its balustraded staircase was strewn with bodies. It was hard to distinguish, at that distance, between the red shirts of the Legion's officers and the red trousers of the enemy, but most of the still figures wore the dark uniforms of the Italian rank and file.

MacWhirter read his gloomy thoughts.

'Ay,' he said, 'the best part of them are ours. You see how it is? The French took the Pamfili in their first rush at dawn. Then they came across the wee burn between——'

'I remember it.'

'And now they're in the Corsini too. I told you, the Corsini is the key to the whole position. Yon house dominates the gate, the walls, everything. Garibaldi knows it. He's *got* to recapture the Corsini. He's sent in wave after wave — but look at the position!'

The problem was laid out, all too clearly, at their feet — and in any case Mark had walked over the actual ground before.

The Corsini grounds ran down the slope towards the city in the shape of a triangle. The apex was formed by the tall pillared gates, from which the drive, hemmed by dense box hedges, went straight up to the villa. Those gates were a fatal bottle-neck through which the Italians had to charge in a compact mass, while French sharpshooters poured down a blistering fire from the cover of the windows and the terrace.

'No wonder,' muttered MacWhirter, 'they're calling it the "angle of Death".'

139

The incredible thing was that the Italians still seemed eager to rush through those fatal gates to almost certain destruction. As Mark watched, sick with the horror of it yet too fascinated to look away, the charge was sounded and a fresh wave of legionaries was flung into the counter-attack.

Nino Bixio himself led the way, an impetuous red-shirted figure with a flashing sabre, riding ahead of the bayonets. He passed the gates. It seemed unbelievable that neither horse nor man was hit. He went on up the drive. The balustrade and shuttered windows spat fire, men dropped as they ran, but the horseman never faltered.

'He's riding up the steps!' Mark gasped.

And it was true. The sure-footed charger seemed to sail up between the marble balusters. Bixio was on the

terrace itself. His sabre flailed down to left and right. Behind him, yelling like madmen, the infantry pounded up the twin staircases.

'He's gone inside!' cried MacWhirter.

And that too was true. Horse and man had disappeared through the tall french windows. Close at their heels swept the legionaries. For a minute or two things went strangely quiet. There was no more firing from the villa. The struggle was raging inside, too far away for much noise to reach the distracted watchers on the wall.

'They've done it then,' said Mark, 'they've got back the Corsini!'

'Wait.'

MacWhirter's dour warning was justified. The musketry

began to crackle as fiercely as ever. In little clusters the Italians started to reappear on the terrace and to drop back, some running, some limping, some staggering. It was as though the bullet-scarred villa were a sponge which was being squeezed — the dark-uniformed figures came out of doors and windows like drops of liquid, spilling over the terrace. Some stopped and did not move again. Others came on down the sloping drive and trickled to comparative safety beyond the gates at the bottom. Among the last, dismounted now and leaning heavily on a friend, was Bixio.

Garibaldi galloped forward to meet him, careless of the bullets sweeping the open ground. Mark saw how the group of officers had dwindled. Daverio, the chief of staff, was gone — killed, said MacWhirter, in the early hours. Young Mameli was still there. Aguyar, of course, was in his usual place. But half the others were missing.

Garibaldi's question came clearly to the tense listeners on the rampart above: 'Where are you hit, Captain?'

'In my side.' Bixio's voice was weaker, but distinct. 'I think it will be all right.'

Stretcher-bearers ran forward as he collapsed, and he was carried out of sight into the city. Garibaldi wheeled away to rally the survivors.

'It's suicide,' said MacWhirter. 'When they get into the villa, the French have always plenty of fresh troops to throw them out again. *They've* no angle of death to worry about, their side.'

Bilibin suddenly spoke behind them. They had almost forgotten that he was there. He sounded agitated, his plump hands were clenching and unclenching.

'Mark — my boy——'

'Sir?'

'I have just seen your poor young friend — Pietro——'

Mark's heart seemed to stop. The blood drained from his cheeks. 'Where? Is he——?'

Bilibin waved a hand towards the waste ground inside the city gate. 'I looked down,' he explained, 'and he was being carried across there. That way.' He pointed to the stretcher-party taking Bixio.

'If they're carrying him, he's only wounded,' said Mac-Whirter bluntly. 'It may not be much. Cheer up, laddie. They'll be taking him to the church just down the hill.'

'We had better follow him,' said Bilibin. 'Are you coming, MacWhirter?'

'Sorry, old fellow. I must stay here.'

'Come on, then, Mark.'

Mark felt his arm taken, felt himself guided down the steep stairs leading from the battlements . . . He was dazed. Somehow, in spite of all his fears, he had never quite faced the fact that Pietro might be wounded, perhaps killed. Palestrina, though wildly exciting while it lasted, had been more like a rough game, in which there had been comparatively few casualties and nobody he knew had been really hurt. Garibaldi's other victories had strengthened the illusion that war was a romantic adventure. In the end one's own side always won. The Italian redshirt, like the British redcoat, was fated to triumph over the enemy.

Now he knew otherwise. He had seen the sickening slaughter in the 'angle of Death'. He realised, numbly, that it was only by good luck that Pietro was not lying there, just another limp sack-like body, raked by the volleys of the French, trampled by each successive charge.

They crossed the waste ground to the top of the narrow lane leading down into the city. There they caught up with Bixio. The stretcher-bearers had been forced to stand aside while a column of reinforcements came streaming up the lane. They were the Lombard Bersaglieri, swinging along in perfect order, taking the stiff incline in their rapid stride, their bugles gay and defiant on the morning air. Their colonel, Manara, the young nobleman from Milan, paused to speak to Bixio. The wounded redshirt answered cheerfully, and the dark green column of riflemen swept on.

Once the lane was clear, Bilibin and Mark were able to pass the stretcher-bearers and hurry down. In a few minutes they reached the church. The steps outside were spattered with dark red stains. As they entered, momentarily half-blinded by the change from glaring sunshine to dim gloom, Mark was chiefly conscious of the smell which rose against them like a wall — blood, sweat, vomit.

They halted just inside. He felt Bilibin's hand friendly on his arm. The stretchers were in long rows under the pillars. Here and there figures moved among them, surgeons, priests, nuns, ladies in rustling summer dresses. There was a constant background murmur of voices, groans, the stertorous breathing of the unconscious, the throat-rattle of the dying.

'We must ask somebody,' whispered Bilibin.

But there was no need. A few yards away one of the ladies rose from her knees and they recognized Tessa.

They went over to her. Mark saw that the soldier on the stretcher was Pietro. His eyes were closed. Tessa greeted them quietly, without surprise. She seemed numb. There were ugly stains all down the front of her dress.

'How is he? Is it bad?'

'I don't know, Marco. The doctor said he would come back.'

'How did you get here? I don't understand——'

'I was here hours ago. They wanted girls to help. I — I never expected——' Her voice shook.

Pietro opened his eyes. They all bent over him together.

'Tessa! Marco! And Mr. Bilibin! Where am I?'

'You're safe, Pietro. You're in the church of San Pietro in Montorio.'

'San Pietro? My own Saint. I should be all right then.' They had to strain to catch his words.

The doctor came back. There was an old priest behind him. Tessa whispered huskily in Italian. The doctor muttered something, shrugged his shoulders, and turned to examine the next patient. The priest fell on his knees and began to speak smoothly and rapidly in Latin.

'Pietro——'

Tessa let out that one terrible little cry. Then she began to shake with silent grief. Mark gripped her hand and stood there, appalled, not knowing what to do or say.

On the other side of him Bilibin groaned. Mark heard him speak, whether to himself or to the others it was not clear.

'To be so helpless,' Bilibin said in a low tense voice. 'Men dying . . . and I too a priest . . . but no comfort to any of them . . .'

The priest stood up. He turned to Tessa.

'You know this boy, *signorina*?'

'My brother——'

'Ah, my poor child . . .' Mark could not understand the rest of it. The old man went away and soon they heard him pattering in Latin on the far side of the next pillar.

Pietro's eyes were shut. He spoke only once again. He too had slipped back into Italian.

'*Mama mia!* I have lost my spectacles. I cannot shoot without my spectacles.'

Soon afterwards the doctor looked back, in passing, and drew the blood-stained blanket over Pietro's face.

Chapter Ten

A MESSAGE TO ITALY

'WE cannot leave now,' said Bilibin hopelessly.
They were back at their lodgings. The afternoon heat pressed leaden-heavy on the drawn blinds. The normal siesta stillness was broken by the continuous gunfire from beyond the Tiber.

Mark looked at his tutor with relief. He had been wondering how to say it himself. Bilibin had spared him the trouble. Of course they could not go now, with Pietro dead and Tessa alone. It was unthinkable.

Bilibin, however, had thought of it, *was* thinking of it, with desperate anxiety. As he paced the dim sitting-room his next words showed that Mark had misunderstood him.

'We did not miss our carriage because we were late in getting back. The landlord says it never came. Now there is not a conveyance to be had. I have done all I can. But Heaven knows what your grandmother will say.'

'I don't much care.'

'Mark!'

'I can't help it,' said Mark stormily. 'My friend is lying there dead — and there's Tessa — she's only a girl, she's younger than me——'

147

'Younger than I,' Bilibin corrected him mechanically.

'Oh, bother grammar! And bother Grandmother! If all you can think of is what she's going to say——!' He broke off, too furious for words.

'I am sorry, my boy.' Bilibin spoke meekly now. 'You have had a terrible experience. It was wrong of me not to remember that. But, you know, *I* am not used to these things, either. And just because such terrible things are happening round us, I feel my responsibility very heavily. It drives everything else out of my mind.'

'I know, sir. I apologize.'

Mark was relieved when there was a tap on the door and MacWhirter came in. He flung himself on the sofa. Even in the greenish gloom of the venetian blinds they could see how haggard he was.

'They're still at it. They retook the Corsini again — but they couldn't hold it. The French seem to have endless reserves. It's like a slaughter-yard. I saw those Bersaglieri mown down — horrible. I came away, I couldn't do any more. It needs an artist like Goya. And if I could draw like Goya would my paper use the stuff?' MacWhirter spoke with a tortured bitterness. 'That's not what Papa wants to leave about in the drawing-room in Kensington — pictures of piled bodies, ripped stomachs, trodden faces! It's war, yes, but it's not what the respectable British public want to know about. They just want the flags and the uniforms and the pretty little puffs of cannon-smoke.'

They let him talk on. Bilibin rang the bell and asked the servant to bring tea and something to eat. MacWhirter recovered himself. It was not like him to become emotional, but he had been up since three and only a bowl of coffee had passed his lips. He listened quietly to their own news, Pietro's death and Bilibin's fruitless attempts to get his pupil away to safety.

'You're right, Bilibin, you'll not get out of Rome now. The French are over the river in two places, above and below the town.'

'Then we can only hang out the Union Jack on our balcony and trust to Providence.'

'Och, you'll be all right. It's what everyone else is doing. What more *can* you do?'

The two men went on talking. Mark only half-listened. They seemed to be in a world apart from himself. They saw things so differently — sometimes they didn't see things at all — they weren't *involved*, somehow. Bilibin still saw Rome as a huge museum of antiquities and the modern inhabitants as tiresome foreigners whose wars and revolutions interfered with study. And Mac-Whirter, his outburst over, was the neutral journalist again, seeing the awfulness of the slaughter but not seeing why all those young men had been ready to die in the gardens of the Corsini.

Suddenly Mark knew, with utter clarity, what he must do.

'Sir——'

'Yes, my boy?'

'That promise I gave you. It's . . . finished now. Isn't it?'

'What do you mean?' The alarm in Bilibin's voice showed that he had a good idea of what Mark meant.

'I said I wouldn't go off with Pietro again. I can't

very well — can I? Pietro's dead. But I can go instead of Pietro.'

'Mark! I realise you are upset today, it has been enough to unbalance anybody. But you must understand — you are in my charge and I absolutely forbid you——'

'All right, sir. You forbid me. You have to. I know that. Grandmother. But suppose I disobey you? What can you do about it?'

Bilibin goggled, his mouth silently opening and shutting. The pale filtered light increased his resemblance to a fish in a tank.

'Disobey me?' he said at last. 'You mean — openly defy me?'

'Not defy, sir. I see your point of view — you can't very well give me permission. But I'm old enough to have a point of view myself. I can't stand out of this. I've got to be in it. I apologize in advance, sir, but, with all due respect, I just have to disobey you.'

MacWhirter let out a croak of laughter. 'I'm sorry, old fellow — don't mean to undermine your authority — but I've never heard such a dignified manifesto of independence!'

Bilibin ignored his friend. He stood up and faced Mark. 'I cannot possibly allow this.'

'But how can you stop me, sir?'

Bilibin hesitated. MacWhirter broke in again.

'He's got you there. You can't lock him in his room.'

'There must be a way. I can go to the British Consul.'

'I doubt if he can help you — even if he wants to. He's very sympathetic to the Republic. Anyhow, he can't prevent British subjects from fighting for it.'

'But Mark is so young——'

'No younger than some of those boys who were up there today.'

'If Mark enlists again,' said Bilibin desperately, 'I shall take up the matter at the highest level. I shall go personally to Mr. Mazzini — or General Garibaldi——'

'D'you think they've nothing better to do than talk to you?'

'They will care for public opinion in England——'

'Public opinion? Bah! The Republic is fighting for its life. One more man on the walls firing a musket is more use to it than all the M.P.s in Westminster. Listen, both of you.' MacWhirter rose from the sofa and came over. 'Will you listen to plain sense? First you, Bilibin.'

'Well?'

'You might just as well save your breath forbidding the laddie anything. You can't stop him doing whatever he sets his mind to do. But you can take comfort from this: the whole thing will be over very quickly. The French have the Corsini and they won't lose it now. They can bombard the city. They've got the guns they hadn't got a month ago. They have the men. The Republic's doomed. So, provided Mark is reasonably lucky, he'll be out of uniform again almost as soon as he's in. And now, laddie,' he went on grimly, turning to Mark, 'I've a word to say to you.'

'I'm listening, sir.'

'You've heard what I've said to Mr. Bilibin. It's all hopeless. That's sober, military fact. You can't do a bit of good. You can upset Mr. Bilibin — maybe you can

get yourself hurt or even killed. You've seen for yourself today. It *could* happen. What's the point, then? It
wouldn't alter the result. Well, what do you say?'

'I'm very sorry, sir. I — I know you've been to lots
of wars and you understand military facts and everything.
But — you *were* wrong about Rome, the first time,
weren't you? I think I shall go along and enlist, just the
same.'

It looked as though MacWhirter had been wrong
again. The first three weeks of sweltering June went by,
but the French seemed no nearer taking the city. From
the cracked remnants of the Villa Corsini their batteries
raked the Porta San Pancrazio and its flanking bastions,
but the defenders clung grimly to their posts along the
sandbagged walls. They even managed to hold some of
the outlying houses and link them with trenches into a
system of forward posts. So long as these remained
intact, the French could not make a frontal assault on the
gateway.

In those three weeks Mark grew up by something
more like three years.

He now wore, proudly, the red shirt of the Legion —
it had become a general issue, no longer marking the
veterans of South American days. Not many of them,
indeed, were still alive. But he was delighted to find that
his own friends of the Palestrina episode, Jacques Duval
and Lorenzo Bellotti, had come through the furnace of
the third of June without harm. They were now seasoned
legionaries and welcomed him joyfully to the ranks.
Perhaps, thought Mark, there was the same unspoken

idea in all their minds, that he was stepping into the gap Pietro had left.

Those were hard, long days under the pitiless sun. There were trenches to be dug, sandbags filled, shattered bricks and rubble banked up again in barricades. Mark looked down to see that his white chest had turned to copper, his aching arms thickened with muscles he had not known he possessed. His own body looked like a stranger's. And this voice — this stream of ungrammatical but ever more confident Italian pouring from his dry and blistered lips — did it really come from Grandmother's delicate boy?

It was not all hard manual labour. There were other duties too. True, he took part in no romantic, suicidal bayonet-charges. There *were* some blood-thirsty raids at night, but these were left to the fully-trained and experienced men. Mark's fighting consisted of long hours in the line, firing a shot at intervals when the chance offered. There were spells as sentry, too, and he was often chosen to carry messages.

'You are English,' explained his company commander with a smile.

'What difference does that make, sir?'

'You are not lazy. You run. Also — forgive me — you do not yet speak Italian easily.'

'Is that an advantage?'

'But of course! These other boys would stop to gossip on the way. And they would not be satisfied to deliver the note I gave them — they would wish to add impressions and suggestions of their own, and these could be very misleading!'

Mark smiled back, though he had a suspicion that often he was made the messenger because he was the youngest and they wanted to keep him out of the firing line. Actually there was nothing specially safe about the job. The French mortar-shells were apt to land anywhere — right down by the river he saw a woman seize one before it could explode and hurl it into the water. And any trip to headquarters was likely to be full of excitement: when not touring all the hottest corners of the front, Garibaldi was usually to be found in a little watch-tower high on the roof of the Villa Savorelli, just inside the gates, and as it commanded the best view of the French positions it was also most exposed to their fire.

He did not see much of Tessa in those feverish weeks when it was commonplace to do twenty-four-hour spells and longer in the line without relief. She was still with the English family but all her spare moments were spent nursing the wounded. The Quirinal Palace was full of convalescent soldiers and a number of English and American ladies worked there. Among them was Bilibin's admired Miss Ellis — but even MacWhirter made no teasing comment when Bilibin joined the helpers. He knew, as Mark knew, that the curate was deeply moved by the suffering around him. Since there was nothing he could do as a priest, the men being either devout Catholics or in a few cases unbelievers, he was eager to make himself useful in the humblest ways.

'And he hasn't so much time to worry about you — or Grandma Apperley,' said MacWhirter with a twinkle in his eye. 'Hard work's a great help. The wee lassie's finding that.'

On the few occasions when Mark saw Tessa he was struck by the way she too had grown older. She was quieter, and that was not just because she was usually, like himself, overtired. She showed no bitterness for Pietro's death, she was intensely proud of him, and she believed as fervently as ever in the cause of Italian liberty.

There was one difference, though. She no longer had the same uncritical admiration for Mazzini. It was to Garibaldi she now turned. If Garibaldi had been given full power, she said, it would have been a different story. Everyone in Rome now knew that Mazzini and Garibaldi disagreed. Mark found to his surprise that Tessa was whole-heartedly for the General.

He himself caught a brief glimpse of that disagreement.

He had been sent with a message to headquarters. He found Garibaldi at his favourite observation-post on the roof of the Villa Savorelli. Garibaldi greeted him with a smile of recognition and a wave of his cigar.

'Ah, my young English friend!'

He always addressed Mark in English, though he knew very little and his accent was bad. He had somehow convinced himself that Mark's Italian was even scantier.

'Wait . . .' He frowned over the dispatch and then over the map in front of him. He had scribbled only the first words of an order when there were voices outside and Mazzini arrived, a trifle breathless from running the

gauntlet of the French snipers. The two leaders shook hands, but a little distantly, it seemed to Mark. Mazzini accepted one of the General's cigars. They plunged then into a brisk and not very cordial discussion. Mark hesitated, then took a step towards the door.

'Wait,' said Garibaldi. He nodded grimly towards the bullet-chipped roof outside the little turret. 'The French — they shoot.'

Mark needed no telling. The French riflemen knew how much Garibaldi used the place and they watched for him. To stand outside would be polite, but it would not be healthy.

The General turned back to Mazzini and relapsed into Italian. 'The boy is English. He understands nothing.' Mazzini looked round and smiled, his first sign of recognition.

'Ah, *you*! I remember now,' he said in English.

Then the two men resumed their argument and forgot Mark's existence.

Much of their vibrant vehement Italian was beyond him, but certain phrases, repeated time and time again for emphasis, were easy to grasp.

'We must fight to the last. There must be no talk of surrender.' That, surprisingly, was the gentle, frock-coated statesman speaking.

'I do not talk of surrender . . . But I am a practical man . . . I do not ask men to die for nothing. Not even soldiers. As for the people in the streets, no!'

'How can you say "die for nothing"? They die for Italy!'

Garibaldi tossed his mane of red-gold hair and ran his finger over the map, explaining rapidly. Mazzini seemed scarcely to listen to the military details. The next thing Mark caught was Garibaldi's concluding remark:

'In such a situation the defence of Rome would become an impossibility.'

The answer was so unexpected that at first he thought he must have misunderstood it. Mazzini said quietly:

'The defence of Rome has always been an impossibility. From the first.'

'No!'

'Yes, General. Once the French seriously decided to take the city I knew it was hopeless. They are the greatest military power in Europe. They cannot risk the humiliation of failure. They will go on — more men, more guns — until they win.'

'Yet you talk of resistance to the last cartridge? You want to see the whole city a heap of ruins, a shambles of blood? Why? In the name of Heaven, *why*?'

'Because the heroic resistance of Rome is demonstrating to the world that we are sincere in our beliefs. Every cause must have its martyrs.'

'Italy has had martyrs! Half my friends are dead! Italy needs rifles — and living hands to use them.'

'I am sorry we cannot see these questions in the same way, General.'

'We never shall!'

It was not a cheerful conversation to overhear.

By the twenty-first of June the long bombardment was beginning to show results. At three points south of the Porta San Pancrazio the walls had been pulverised until now, instead of rising like cliffs, they offered fan-shaped slopes of rubble, like slag-heaps. Elsewhere the Janiculum and the Trastevere quarter below were dotted with ruins and the Villa Savorelli was itself a lace-pattern of shot-holes. But Garibaldi still climbed every morning to his perilous look-out, unconcernedly puffing his cigar. Every morning the French snipers greeted him with their rifles, and every morning they failed to do more than chip the tiles.

In the early hours of the twenty-second Mark was roused by Jacques violently shaking his arm. It was still dark. There was a little firing, but not much, and some distance away. With an effort he struggled back to consciousness.

'What's happened?'

'I don't know. But we have to stand to.'

They soon heard what had happened, and the news was not good. The French had captured the two bastions in the southern sector which their siege-guns had already breached. This part of the defences had been entrusted to one of the old Papal regiments, who had fought bravely throughout the last two or three weeks. But now they seemed to have panicked. Waking from the sleep of exhaustion — and Mark could sympathise with them there — the soldiers had found the French bayonets almost at their throats. After a brief resistance they had bolted. The French now held several hundred yards of the wall.

'They should send in the Legion to counter-attack,' said Bellotti excitedly. 'We could soon throw them out before they establish themselves and bring up their guns.'

'Could we?' said the Belgian.

'Are you afraid?'

'No. Yes,' Jacques corrected himself with an apologetic laugh, 'but I would go if I was ordered. Nevertheless, it would be suicide. And remember, my friend, one can only commit suicide once!'

'The General hasn't much use for suicide,' said Mark. 'Nobody suggests that *he* is afraid.'

The order soon came to move, but not to counter-attack. Instead, there was to be a new defence-line. The Porta San Pancrazio and the ramparts north of it were still safely held, but to the south the troops were to take up a position along the remains of the ancient wall, built by the Emperor Aurelian, which ran slanting downhill towards the Trastevere. It hinged on to the more modern fortifications quite close to the gate, and, though far from ideal, formed an inner barrier which the French had not bargained for.

'It's the beginning of the end,' prophesied MacWhirter as he crouched beside Mark, sketching the altered scene.

'You've said that before, sir.' Mark tried to sound jaunty but his heart was heavy. He remembered the conversation he had heard between Mazzini and Garibaldi. He would have liked very much to discuss it with the Scotsman but he dared not. MacWhirter was a journalist. Mark must not pass on anything he had picked up at headquarters.

'Listen, laddie. Old Bilibin and I are getting worried about you——'

'Again? I'm all right.'

'I mean when the French finally get in.' MacWhirter kept his voice low. 'It may be messy.'

'It may. *If.*'

'They will. Now: when that moment comes you'll have done all you can and — supposing you're still safe and sound — there's no sense in getting killed. Upsetting for old Bilibin. Vexatious for this dreadful old grandmother of yours. So . . . ' MacWhirter glanced round furtively and then passed him a slip of paper. Mark saw an embossed heading and a few scribbled lines in English and French, signed by the British Consul. 'Stow that away somewhere safe,' MacWhirter ordered. 'No, no, not in the pocket of your shirt! You've got to get rid of this red garment, first thing you do.'

'Look, sir,' Mark began indignantly, 'if you expect me to——'

'I don't expect you to do anything dishonourable. I *do* expect you not to do anything stupid. This is a last resort. If a time comes when nobody's giving you any more orders and you just have to look after yourself . . . I've seen an army in rout. It's not a pretty sight. If that time comes, make for your lodgings. If the French catch you, wave this paper at them. But remember, they won't be very impressed if you're still wearing a red shirt and a floppy hat and looking like a Calabrian brigand!'

Mark had to laugh. He put away the document, feeling a little ashamed of possessing it, yet unwilling to throw it back in MacWhirter's face. The Scotsman read what was in his mind.

'You'd be surprised,' he murmured, 'what a lot o' these passes are being handed round — and not only to British subjects! Mr. Freeborn is very, very sympathetic to the Republic — perhaps it's his name. And Mr. Brown won't let the United States be outdone by Her Britannic Majesty.'

'Thank you, sir. Tell Mr. Bilibin not to worry. If the worst comes to the worst . . . ' Mark paused significantly.

'Sensible laddie.'

MacWhirter closed his sketch-book and departed, bending his lanky body almost double to avoid the French bullets which kept whistling over the top of the wall.

Four days later Mark was sent with another message for the General, who had moved his headquarters to the Villa Spada further down the hillside and closer to the new Aurelian line. He saluted and held out the dispatch. Garibaldi was about to take it. Then, suddenly, the outstretched hand was withdrawn and the General was out of his chair and round the table in one wild rush.

'*Anita!*'

'Peppino!'

Startled, Mark turned. In the doorway stood a young woman, fine-featured and very dark. That was all he saw before she was engulfed in the General's massive embrace. He heard their voices, muffled as they clung together.

'I had just written to you — I thought you were in Nice!'

'I had to come, Peppino!'

'The children?'

'The children are fine. Your mother is looking after them. I tell you, I had to come. My place is with you.'

That was Mark's first sight of Signora Garibaldi. Later he realised that her dramatic arrival was all of a piece with her life and character.

She and Garibaldi had met in her native South America, fallen in love at sight, and eloped together. For years she had shared his adventures on the pampas. After one battle, thinking him dead, she had ridden for sixty miles alone, across tropical forest, mountain-pass, and flooded river, running the gauntlet of the enemy. At another time she had had to escape with him carrying her twelve-day baby on her saddle-bow.

It was just like Anita Garibaldi, when the news was blackest, to leave her children in a place of safety and slip through the enemy lines to be with her husband.

Garibaldi needed any consolation he could find during that tragic final week of June. Mark, for the rest of his life, never experienced a midsummer heat-wave without remembering those days. Torrid sunshine and azure skies were forever associated with blood and death. Even darkness brought little relief. The French mortars continued to lob their bombs into the city — their curving flight could be traced by the glow of the fuse until it dived below the housetops and was followed by a muffled explosion. And there was always the knowledge that soon, perhaps tonight, perhaps tomorrow night, the French might launch another of their attacks.

The twenty-ninth was the feast-day of St. Peter and St. Paul. It was amazing, thought Mark, that even at a time like this the gay Romans would not miss the excuse for a *festa*. He squatted on the Aurelian Wall that night, his back against the comfortingly solid sandbags, and looked over the city, twinkling with candles, murmurous with distant laughter and song. The dome of St. Peter's, brilliantly illuminated, hung low over the horizon like some distorted harvest-moon. From time to time rockets went hissing skywards, to come tumbling down again in a shower of coloured beauty.

Grandmother would have sneered and talked of 'frivolous foreigners'. Mark wasn't sure whether or not to admire a people who were prepared to celebrate their usual *festa*, come what might, and would not let all the artillery in the French Army lessen their pleasure in a firework display.

Midnight brought a sudden, sharp rainstorm, which sent the late revellers to shelter and left the city almost in darkness, save for the lights on St. Peter's dome. There was a refreshing smell of wet earth and reviving foliage. The last thing he remembered, as he lay down to sleep in his half-soaked clothes, was the sudden pang of homesickness for Worcestershire and all the garden-scents there.

He was not allowed to sleep for long. At two o'clock they all had to stand to arms. The French were moving in to the kill. Out of the starless night brimmed a tide of men and steel.

From that moment, till sunrise, it was a nightmare. The struggle raged along the Aurelian Wall, over the

waste ground by the gateway, all round the ruins of the
Villa Savorelli. Like a true nightmare it left only confused and fragmentary impressions behind — of shouting, shoving, firing, reloading, stumbling, falling, being
kicked, scrambling up again. The creeping dawn-light
only emphasised the confusion. Units were all mixed up
together. Mark found himself fighting beside stray Bersaglieri, a Polish volunteer in his strange square-crowned
cap, and one of Masina's lancers, dismounted, thrusting at the French with his lance like some ancient
warrior.

Then, suddenly, there was Garibaldi just in front, he
too like an ancient warrior, some hero out of the *Iliad*,
his sabre rising and falling, his black ostrich-feathers
tossing amid the shakoes of the enemy.

'Come on!' he bellowed. 'This is the last fight!'

Mark and the others plunged after him, and for the
time being they seemed irresistible. Mark lost sight of
the General but for a little while he could still hear his
voice. He was singing. He was roaring out *Fratelli
d'Italia*. So at the moment when young Mameli was
dying of his wounds in the hospital a mile or two
away, his battle-song was rallying the defence to a final
effort.

They did in fact recover the Aurelian Wall as the
dawn broke. They crouched there behind their battered,
tumbled defences, those who were left, and endured the
constant fire of the enemy. The French seemed to be
busier elsewhere. The hottest fighting was round the
northern bastion and what was left of the Villas Savorelli
and Spada. At noon, when Mark was almost asleep

on his feet, the firing died away and the bugles rang out.

'A truce,' muttered Bellotti.

Mark groaned.

'Come on!' The young journalist was shaking him. 'They say we can go out and bring in the wounded. Poor Jacques is out there in the sun.'

'Of course!' Mark blinked, pulled himself together and clambered to his feet. Somehow one always had a little extra strength when it was absolutely necessary ... He followed Bellotti; they picked their way among the crumpled bodies, to where the Belgian lay. He was still alive and conscious. There was a lot of blood, but it was all on his leg. Bellotti bandaged him hurriedly, Mark managed to find a couple of stretcher-bearers, and their friend was soon on his way to hospital. French and Italians were mingling freely, picking up their wounded and dead.

Back on the wall, Mark asked: 'How long will the truce last?'

Bellotti shrugged his shoulders. 'Who knows? They say the General has ridden off to the Capitol. The Assembly is meeting. They will have to decide something. Quickly.'

Pails of tepid coffee and baskets of bread came round. They took their small rations avidly, then stretched out in what shade the parapet provided. The hot afternoon passed, for Mark, in blissful unconsciousness. The person who woke him next time was MacWhirter.

'Thank the Lord you're all right!'

'Oh — hullo, sir! What's — what's happening? I——'

'I've just come from the Assembly. Mazzini wanted to fight on, as I knew he would — let the Republic go down in some heroic, hopeless sort of blood-bath. "A message to Italy", he called it.'

'What did the General say?'

'I admire that man,' said MacWhirter, and Mark knew that those few gruff words meant as much as other people's eloquence. 'You know he stood up there in the Assembly just as he'd come from the battle. Blood all over his uniform. Sword so bent it wouldn't go right down into his scabbard. If ever a man had cause to despair — you know, by the way, the negro's dead?'

'Aguyar? No.'

'Killed by a shell in the Trastevere. You may think that's nothing much — just one more of his friends. But it shook him. He was told as he came into the meeting. Anyhow, I was telling you. He spoke out against Mazzini. There was no sense in giving Rome over to destruction. On the other hand, he said he'd never surrender.'

'What else can he do?'

'Take to the hills, he says. As he used to do in South America. Rome is more than just a place, he says, it's a spirit. He said something rather fine, I thought. "Wherever *we* go," he said, "there Rome will be!" They cheered like anything. And then,' added MacWhirter, reverting to his old cynical tone, 'they voted for surrender. I'll say this for Mazzini — he got up and supported Garibaldi's plan, and when the surrender motion was carried instead, he resigned on the spot.'

'Good for him!'

'So — it's all over. The French won't march in to-day, perhaps not even tomorrow. These matters take time to arrange. Plenty of time to change your shirt, laddie!'

'I'm not altogether sure I want to change it,' Mark answered slowly.

MacWhirter's blue eyes narrowed. 'I hope you're going to be sensible,' he said.

Chapter Eleven

WHO IS FOR THE HILLS?

THE French were to occupy the city on July the third. Under their protection a government of three cardinals was to replace the democratic republic. But first, on the day before, all those who preferred not to surrender but to march out into the wilderness with Garibaldi were invited to meet him in front of St. Peter's.

The great piazza was thronged. 'Twelve thousand, I'd say,' grunted MacWhirter, peering round, 'though for every one who wants to go with Garibaldi there are probably two trying to persuade him not to! Phew! No use getting out my sketch-book in this crush——'

'But your editor will want a picture of this,' cried Tessa. 'It will be an historic scene!'

'No doubt. And I shall draw it — when all the people have gone. I know what the General looks like, and Ugo Bassi, and one or two more. For the rest of the twelve thousand I can use my imagination — the editor doesn't expect portraits of the lot.'

'Always you are cynical, Mr. MacWhirter!'

'Practical, lassie, a practical journalist.'

'Look,' Mark interrupted. He pointed across the sea of heads filling the square below the steps on which they were standing. Hats and handkerchiefs were waving. A lonely figure on a horse was edging slowly forward towards the tall Egyptian obelisk in the centre. The cries of '*Viva Garibaldi!*' thundered louder and were echoed back from the walls of the great church and the encircling colonnades.

It took some minutes for the rider to reach the obelisk, so many people wanted to speak to him or shake his hand. At last a way was cleared. He greeted the officers clustered round the plinth and raised his hand for silence. Slowly, from the centre outwards, the storm of cheering died away. Across the gulf of stillness came the deep, measured tones.

'Fortune, who deserts us today, will smile on us tomorrow . . . I am going out from Rome. . . . Those who wish to carry on the struggle against the foreigner, let them come with me!'

The cheering broke out again, but the red-sleeved arm went up to quell it. Quietly, rather grimly, the voice went on.

'I offer neither pay, nor quarters, nor rations. I offer hunger, thirst, forced marches, battles — and death. He who loves his country in his heart, and not only with his lips, let him follow me.'

This time there was no checking the applause. Garibaldi waited, statuesque on his white horse, merely bending his head to say something to his officers. Then he raised his hand, gained silence, and spoke for the last time.

'Very well. We meet this evening. In front of the Lateran, at six. Long live the Republic!' He waved his hat high in the air. 'Long live Italy!' As the tumult rose again, he moved slowly away across the piazza. Many of the crowd, Mark noticed, were weeping, and not all of them were women.

'Come on,' said MacWhirter briskly, 'we can all do with a cup of coffee — or maybe something stronger, some of us. Let's find a café. I'll go back and sketch the piazza when all these good folk have gone away.'

It seemed a good idea. Mark, for one, felt weak and drained of emotion. Thanks to youth and health, he had made a quick physical recovery from the lost sleep and other hardships of the siege, but his mind was taking longer. He had seen and felt so much. So many problems still warred together in his brain. He wanted to sit down quietly and think — not that there was much chance of calm meditation in that crowded café, with Tessa, Mac-Whirter and Bilibin babbling round the table.

Tessa turned to him now and lowered her voice. She was smiling, excited, and slightly pink.

'Marco——' She tried to sound casual. 'I have a great favour to ask.'

'Anything, Tessa.'

'Have you a spare pair of trousers you could lend me? Give me, really.'

The effect of this remark was startling. Bilibin choked and spilt his coffee over his own trousers — though he would never have called them that in a lady's hearing. To hear a lady herself use the word 'trousers' with such matter-of-fact frankness, rather than referring coyly to 'nether garments' or 'inexpressibles', was a shock for which he was not prepared.

Even Mark was taken aback. It was, he told himself quickly, just another of those cases where Tessa, though she had grown up with a good working knowledge of the English language, had never mastered the finer points of usage in refined society.

'Er . . . yes . . . of course. Do you want them taken to the hospital?' He assumed that she wanted them for some young convalescent whose own 'nether garments' were too torn or blood-stained to be worn again.

'The hospital?' She knitted her brows in puzzlement. 'I have finished there. No, no, Marco. For myself.'

'*For yourself?*' they all said in unison. Even MacWhirter found it necessary to take a hasty gulp of brandy.

'Signora Garibaldi is going to dress like a man. If I am to go with her, she says I too must have trousers. I still have poor Pietro's clothes, but they are so big. And though Marco *is* bigger than me——'

For once Bilibin let the grammatical error pass. He cried:

'My dear girl, you're not going with the soldiers?'

'Yes. Signora Garibaldi is going. She has persuaded the General.' Tessa laughed. 'Even the General cannot give orders to the Signora! Oh, she is a wonderful woman. I have talked to her when she came to see the wounded. She says I can go, she is finding me a horse — but the trousers I must find for myself!'

MacWhirter leant forward. 'Lassie, do you realise what you're letting yourself in for?'

'I heard the General just now. "Hunger, thirst, forced marches, battles — and death." '

'Ay. And he wasn't exaggerating. But he didn't tell you all the details. See here.' MacWhirter's bony fingers moved deftly over the table, shifting cups and glasses to illustrate his points. 'Here's Rome. Here's the French, twenty or thirty thousand of them. Over here, the Spaniards — och, I know they've done nothing yet, but they're not far away, six thousand of 'em, and they'll try to be in at the death. By the same token, Naples has twelve thousand men under arms — they'd like to wipe out the shame of Palestrina and Velletri, I don't doubt, and they're so jealous of the French they'd dearly love to gain the credit for finishing Garibaldi. Suppose he turns north and gives them all the slip? Fifteen thousand Austrians are ready for him — here, in Florence, here, in Perugia, here, on the Adriatic coast at Ancona . . . och, I haven't enough cups and glasses to mark them all.'

'Never mind, Mr. MacWhirter. It makes no difference.'

'But why, lassie, *why*?'

Tessa's eyes flashed. 'Because I will not stay in Rome and watch the French march in tomorrow. Because I will not see the old corruptions and injustices brought back — the spying, the censorship, the political prisoners.' She hesitated, and then added: 'I think I am also going because the Signora should not go without some other woman to keep her company. She is to have another child.' Without waiting for their reactions, Tessa got to her feet. 'I have not much time, Marco. May I walk back with you for the trousers? And then——' There was a catch in her voice. 'And then I think it will be time to say good-bye.'

'Not to me,' said Mark. He looked across at Bilibin. 'If Tessa goes to look after Signora Garibaldi, *I'm* going to look after Tessa.'

The clocks in the city were striking six. The vast shadow of the Lateran Palace was creeping across the piazza to the eastern gate through which the column was to leave. In that shadow — and, as it seemed to Mark, in another even deeper shadow, the shadow perhaps of death itself — the men were mustering.

It was going to be a small army. No more than twice the force which had marched to Palestrina. Four thousand, say — four thousand against all the tens of thousands MacWhirter had so gloomily totted up on the other side. The bulk were redshirts, Garibaldi's own

faithful followers. There were the Lombard Bersaglieri
too, their trimly tailored uniforms now much the worse
for wear, their numbers down to a hundred or two —
their colonel and many of their comrades had died in the
last fierce struggle for the Villa Spada. There were a few
survivors of Masina's lancers and several hundred
dragoons of the old papal cavalry.

The artillery consisted of one small cannon. There
were a few waggons laden with ammunition and supplies.

Among the clustered riders near by Mark could see
Anita Garibaldi and Tessa. In their red shirts they were
hard to distinguish from the officers. They were chatting
with Ugo Bassi. The friar was mounted on a lively
English thoroughbred, which (Lorenzo Bellotti explained) had been given him by Garibaldi so that he
could always keep up with the General.

Mark was glad that Lorenzo was going too.

'But of course, Marco! How could I stay? There will
be no life for a journalist in Rome once the old gang are
back, censoring and suppressing the newspapers.'

It was sad that they were leaving Jacques in hospital,
but with luck he would be all right. The French would
treat him properly and, when he was recovered, his
Belgian nationality should protect him from the ven-
geance of the new government. For Romans, and for
other Italians, it was a blacker prospect.

'Mazzini is staying,' said Lorenzo. 'That is brave,
but I think it is foolish.'

'Why doesn't he come with us?'

'That also would be foolish. Mazzini is no soldier. He
and Garibaldi together? No. He should go back to

London and wait until he can be useful again. But he will not run away.' Lorenzo shook his head. 'It is dangerous, though.'

It was a quiet, businesslike scene, very different from the emotional gathering earlier in the day. Officers moved through the ranks, checking numbers, arms and equipment. Though the volunteers fell into natural groups of old comrades every unit had to be re-formed. The only raised voices were those of distracted relatives and friends, weeping and arguing in a last attempt to dissuade men from joining such a forlorn venture. Some of the youngest redshirts were dodging about in a furtive manner to avoid their parents.

'And your tutor,' inquired Lorenzo, 'this kind of English priest who travels with you — what did *he* say?'

'Oh, we had all the same arguments over again. Poor old Bilibin! I don't like upsetting him.'

'Naturally, he is upset. Is he not responsible for you to the old lady, your grandmother?'

'Yes, that's what worries him. But I told him, since he can't control me, the logical thing is to resign the post, here and now. I have written a letter to my grandmother and given it to him. Just in case anything happens to me. And MacWhirter will bear out the story. Bilibin can't be blamed. He's finished with me. He ought to be glad,' Mark added, 'I've been a constant source of worry to him. Now he's free. Perhaps he'll ask Miss Ellis to marry him.'

Lorenzo laughed. 'That is something I can never get used to! That a priest can marry! Ah, I think I see your Mr. MacWhirter——'

'He's sure to be here. He'll want to sketch the scene for his paper. I only hope,' said Mark anxiously, turning his head, 'that he hasn't got Bilibin in tow. I don't want that argument all over again.'

'No, no, he has a soldier with him.'

'A soldier?' Mark stared aghast. He had picked out the tall figure of the Scotsman moving through the crowd, conspicuous among the slighter Italian figures in their uniforms. Sure enough, it was a red shirt his companion was wearing, but — 'That's not a soldier,' Mark exclaimed, '*it's Bilibin!*'

Before he could recover from his amazement the two men had seen him and were at his side. Bilibin was a fantastic spectacle. He wore his red shirt blouse-fashion, like many of the others, flopping down outside his trousers and masking the comfortable curve of his stomach. On his head was his usual top-hat, on his back an immense bulging knapsack. He carried his musket in the crook of his arm, rather as if he were going out after pheasant, and in his belt was a terrifying dagger.

'They gave me these,' he stammered. 'They insisted. Of course I cannot *use* them. As a clerk in Holy Orders I cannot shed blood. I could not explain — nobody spoke English — I was afraid that if I did not take what they gave me, I should not be allowed to come——'

'But — sir! You're not coming with us?'

'He is,' said MacWhirter.

'But you're not interested in Italian freedom——'

'That is beside the point,' said Bilibin. 'Where you go, I must go. That is my duty as I see it.'

'It's ridiculous! There's no need. I told you, sir,

178

you've only to resign — then you've no further obligation.'

Bilibin shook his head. For all his outlandish get-up he seemed to take on a new dignity.

'My dear boy,' he said quietly, 'duties are not something we can lay down, at a moment's notice, just when they become difficult. Mrs. Apperley is not here to accept my resignation. There is no one to whom I can pass over my responsibility. So . . . there it is.'

'I . . . I'm truly sorry, sir.'

'You too must do your duty — as you see it.' Bilibin fumbled in his trouser-pocket and brought out a couple of letters, which he handed to MacWhirter. 'This one is for Mrs. Apperley — but keep it and post it only if — if there is need.'

'I understand,' said the Scotsman gruffly.

'And this is for Miss Ellis——'

'Ay.'

'Emphasise how distressed I was that I had no time to call and make my farewells in person. Say that I hope I shall someday have the pleasure of meeting her — and of course the other ladies — again. But I have said all that in the letter. You had better go now, my dear MacWhirter, and get your sketches done before the column moves off.' He gripped his friend's hand.

Mark broke in on their farewell. 'Mr. MacWhirter, he *can't* go. He doesn't realise what it will be like. The marching will kill him.'

MacWhirter looked down with a stony expression. 'Don't be too sure. There's a lot o' things about Mr. Bilibin that would surprise you.' He shook hands with Mark. 'I hope you're satisfied with what you've done.'

Mark did not know what to say. MacWhirter continued dryly: 'If Miss Ellis were a Highland woman I'd have said she had the sight.'

'The sight? You mean — second sight? Why?'

'Weeks ago she said you were a Perpetual Problem. And so you are. Good-bye, then, and good luck to you.'

He turned and strode away, opening his sketch-book. He was just in time. Officers were beginning to call their contingents to attention. Soon the column began to uncoil, snake-like, and pass through the Porta San Giovanni into the sunset-reddened wastes of the Campagna.

'Where are we going?' Bilibin murmured as they tramped through the archway.

'I don't know, sir. The General never says.'

'We are heading east, though.'

Mark laughed. 'With Garibaldi that doesn't mean a thing.'

Chapter Twelve

ARMY OF SHADOWS

AND where *were* they going?

'I just didn't think much,' Mark was to say long afterwards. 'You don't at that age. It was all so exciting at the time. I suppose I lived for the moment.' And he would add, with a rueful laugh: 'If I'd been older and had more experience — if I'd known half of what was in store for us — I'd have been in such a funk I'd most likely have skedaddled. But of course there was Tessa. I'd have felt pretty much of a worm, letting *her* go . . .'

The sun went down behind them, twilight came up

over the land in front. Soon they could no longer see, on distant hillocks, the watchful figures of the mounted patrols, roving far ahead to make sure there were no Spaniards near.

A man in front of Mark brought out a cigar, but before he could light it an officer called out:

'No smoking! General's orders!'

'Here — hang it, the General himself likes a cigar!'

'Not tonight. He will deny himself.'

There was a general groan from the ranks.

'They have all become cigar-smokers — to imitate the General!' whispered Lorenzo scornfully. 'They do not realise, it is not the cigar that makes the hero.'

'Quiet, there! No talking! That too is General's orders.'

They went forward into the gathering shadows, themselves an army of shadows, noiseless save for the dull rhythmic thud of feet, the clop-clop-clop of an officer trotting up and down the column, the creak and rumble of the waggons.

Mark's mind went back to that first night-march in May. No doubt Garibaldi had the same object in view again — to get a flying start, to cross the open plain under cover of darkness, and to reach hill-country by daylight. This time the need for secrecy was even greater. There were more enemies, and more dangerous ones, in the field against him. And there was no longer a base to fall back upon. In a few hours the French tricolour would have replaced the red-white-and-green in Rome.

There were brief halts when even the strictest officers, though they could stop the lighting of a cigar, could

not prevent a little whispered conversation. Half-way
through the night Bilibin murmured:

'We have changed direction. We have doubled back
on our tracks. We were going east to begin with. Now
it is north-west.'

'How do you know, sir?'

'The stars. As a boy I was very interested in
astronomy.'

It was a queer thing about Bilibin, one was always
making unexpected discoveries. It was the same with the
marching. Mark had been dreading that a few hours on
the road would reduce the curate to a state of collapse.
He was relieved — and at the same time just a little
piqued — to discover that Bilibin was still as fresh as, or
even fresher than, himself.

'At Oxford,' Bilibin confessed, 'being too poor to
keep a horse I was extremely fond of pedestrian exercise.
I think I have told you of my tour of the Lakes? I fear
I am badly out of training, but it is a great help to be
walking in the cool of the night.'

As the dawn broke, the countryside took on a familiar
look. Mark recognized the ruins of Hadrian's Villa — so
they were back here again, though by such a roundabout
route that they had doubled their former mileage. To
his dismay the column showed no signs of halting even
now. Did Garibaldi expect them to go on until they died
on their feet?

Relief, however, was near. Another mile or two, by a
steep road winding up the Sabine foothills, brought them
to the gates of Tivoli, clinging to its wooded precipices
above the glittering cataracts of the Anio. Here, just

short of the gates, the longed-for word to halt was given. Eleven hours after leaving Rome they were free to fall out and spread themselves under the olive-trees.

'Tea?' murmured Bilibin invitingly.

Mark stirred, groaned, and sat up, rubbing his eyes. The ground was hard and stony, but he had never slept more soundly at home. For a few moments in fact he had the illusion that he was at home.

'Did you say *tea*, sir?'

'Yes.' Bilibin thrust a steaming mug under his nose. 'I thought as it was nearly four o'clock in the afternoon——'

'Where on earth did you get tea?'

'Oh, I brought it. Coffee is very well, but there are times when only tea will do. I was boiling water for my shave, so I thought, afterwards . . .'

'Marvellous! Thank you very much, sir.' Mark looked at his tutor with gratitude and a new respect.

Bilibin sat back against the grey tree-trunk, his smooth cheeks dappled with leaf-shadows, looking as self-possessed as if he were on a choir-picnic.

'I have been talking to the chaplain, an extraordinarily interesting man——'

'Ugo Bassi? Does he know English?'

'We talked in Latin. A little difficult at first; he uses the Italian pronunciation, of course. . . . However, I soon adjusted myself.'

'What did you talk about?' Mark could not imagine that Bilibin would have much sympathy for the friar's fervent politics and he hoped they had not got on to religion, because Bilibin, to Bassi, must presumably appear a misguided heretic.

'Oh, the classics,' his tutor answered in a surprised tone. What else should they talk about, he seemed to imply? Were they not at Tivoli, the ancient Tibur, with all its memories of Horace and Catullus and Propertius, Marius and Maecenas and Augustus and the rest? 'A most beautiful spot,' continued Bilibin. 'No wonder the Romans built their houses here. One can picture the poet . . .' He lapsed into Latin verse. 'I need not translate?'

'Well, sir . . . my Latin's got a bit rusty this past month.'

'Horace compares himself with a bee,

> *"Sipping each sweet thyme-blossom, wandering*
> *Through the dense groves, athwart the slopes*
> *of Tibur,*
> *So rich in streams . . ."*

Yes, it is delightful here after the heat of the city. There are so many waterfalls, just as there were two thousand years ago. It would be pleasant to stay here for a week or two.'

'Some hope! You don't know Garibaldi.' Mark jumped to his feet and slapped the dusty earth from his trousers. 'I wonder how Tessa stood the journey. Will you excuse me, sir?'

He wandered up through the silvery grove, past a few dozen tiny camp-fires each with its dozing or gossiping group of volunteers, until he came to where the waggons

stood parked outside the gates of the town and a line of
horses whisked their tails in the shade. Almost at once
he saw Tessa on a bench beside Signora Garibaldi. She
did not see him, and for a full minute he hesitated shyly,
until the General's wife raised her head, flashed him a
humorous smile and beckoned him forward.

'You are the English boy, Marco, yes? I have heard
of you.'

'Good day, *signora*. Hullo, Tessa, how are you
feeling?'

She made a face. 'Very stiff! After a few miles I did
not know whether to pity you without a horse — or
envy you!'

The Signora laughed. 'Never mind, little Tessa. After
a day or two you will be a proper *gaucho*.'

Mark saw that Tessa had cut her hair. Now it hung
clear of her shoulders and was shorter than some of the
men's, Garibaldi's included. She wore her red shirt loose
and had already found time and a needle to improve its
fit. It looked, too, as though she had taken an inch or
two off the trouser-legs. With a pistol at her belt and a
soft-crowned hat framing her head she seemed well on
the way to becoming 'a proper *gaucho*' already.

'The long march was worth while, Marco.' She offered
him a telescope. 'Look, you can see the whole plain,
right across to the walls of Rome.'

'Yes. . . .'

'And it is empty still? There are no troops coming
this way?'

Mark scanned the dry landscape at his feet. The road
to the city was clear in all its length. He knew by now

how easy it was to pick out a marching army from its dust-cloud and the glint of its metal in the sun.

'Not a sign.'

'So, you see — we have given them the slip so far. And by the time General Oudinot learns that we are here — pouf, we shall *not* be here!'

'That's what I imagined. Poor old Bilibin was just thinking how pleasant it would be to stay here for a week or two!'

'And how is poor old Bilibin?'

'Fit as a flea. Not poor at all. Not old either. *I* felt about a hundred when I got here this morning.'

The Signora broke in again, speaking her imperfect Italian with its flavour of Brazilian Portuguese: 'The General is coming back — he rode up into the hills somewhere this afternoon. Now perhaps we shall know where we are to sleep tonight — if we sleep at all!'

Mark was not in the least surprised when the match was resumed at six o'clock in the evening. They could not afford to stay there within sight of Rome. The townspeople seemed friendly enough, coming out with wine and fruit and other presents, but behind some of those smiles there was sure to be enmity. It would not be long before the news of their presence in Tivoli filtered through to the French and then there would be dust-clouds on the plain all right.

The road lay east again, climbing higher up the gorge of the Anio, towards the Neapolitan border. As they marched off, there were cheers and jokes from the spectators. They were going to have another slap at

King Bomba, were they? Good luck to them! The volunteers laughed and shouted back promises of what they would do to Bomba if he did not run too fast for them. Garibaldi, riding past to overtake the head of the column, merely waved his hand and smiled an enigmatic smile.

Mark braced himself for another gruelling all-night march, this time uphill. He noticed that Bilibin was no longer carrying a musket.

'Ah, no! The worthy friar has arranged that little matter for me. He too carries no arms, although he wears the red shirt. He appreciates my problem. I shall make myself useful in other ways. I was able to make a little joke of it,' Bilibin added happily, 'turning the well-known Virgilian tag, *Arma virumque cano*. . . . It seemed to go down very well.'

'I'm sure it did.'

'If you get tired during the night, my dear boy, you must allow me to carry yours. That would not constitute "bearing arms" in the legal sense.'

'I shall be all right, thank you, sir.'

However, there was no night-march. They had gone only a few miles when they found themselves wheeling off the highway and received the order to bivouac there on the wooded mountainside.

'But I slept all the morning and half the afternoon,' Lorenzo grumbled. 'How can I sleep now? I wish the General would make up his mind.'

Everybody was perplexed by the change of plan. Had news arrived of some danger in front? Spaniards or Neapolitans? The only thing to do was to curl up as comfortably as possible and get what extra sleep they could. Whatever happened, they could be sure of missing plenty later on.

Reveille came before daylight, though there was no bugle-blowing and no unnecessary noise. Ranks were formed. Several people seemed to be missing in Mark's contingent and at the time he assumed that they were somewhere else in the column, having failed to find their proper places in the dark. Later Lorenzo explained with a shrug of his shoulders:

'We shall not see them again. They have gone home.'

'Home? You mean — they've deserted?'

'Yes.'

'Already!' said Mark scornfully. 'Then why did they ever come?'

'To get out of Rome. Perhaps to gain a little more time to think and decide. Men are of all kinds, Marco. To put on a red shirt does not make one a hero like Garibaldi or a saint like Ugo Bassi. We have our share of cowards — and worse. But do not look so gloomy, we have some good men too. We have not left them all in the hospitals and graveyards of Rome.'

The quality of those men was tested soon enough. The column had not resumed its eastward march up the main road. Again Garibaldi had doubled in his tracks. Mark and his friends, now part of the vanguard, found themselves facing a precipitous shoulder of mountain. The only way up it was a stony, zigzag path, climbing endlessly to the dawn-streaked sky. At the first bend they overtook Garibaldi and a knot of officers, reined in beside a gesticulating shepherd.

'But I swear to you, General — by all the Saints! You will never get your waggons over this mountain. This track is impossible. No cart has ever passed this way——'

'There must be a first time for everything, my friend.'

'It cannot be done, General!'

'It can. It will be. I was here yesterday afternoon.'

'You will not believe me?'

'No. And no one will believe you if you tell them that you have seen an army pass this way. So,' Garibaldi chuckled, 'save your breath, old man. Tell nobody today that you have seen us. Or tomorrow.'

'I understand, General. God go with you!'

'And you.' Garibaldi turned in his saddle and called to the officer in command of Mark's company: 'Take it slowly up here — do not go racing on. We may have a little trouble with the transport.'

It was a masterly understatement. They needed no invitation to take it slowly. The mule-track steepened. The mountain seemed to arch its back against them like an ill-tempered cat at bay. The sun too was climbing. The rays struck hotter and hotter between their shoulder-blades and they needed no other clue to tell them that they were marching west again. The red shirts clung to their bodies, dark and soaked. Bilibin admitted, with his usual refinement of phrase, that he was perspiring to excess. He looked like a strawberry ice in the last stages of collapse.

'Thank goodness we're nowhere near the waggons!' said Mark selfishly. 'Look at them!'

Far below, the waggons were still creeping up the mountainside. Every now and then, one would halt and look as if it had stopped for ever. Shouts and curses would float up through the thin mountain air, then the waggon would jerk forward once more. The troops unlucky enough to be within call had been pressed into service. They were straining, shoving, at times even lifting the jammed wheels over the boulders which obstructed them. But on the waggons came.

'Remarkable!' panted Bilibin. 'I am reminded of Hannibal crossing the Alps.'

You would be, thought Mark, and *I* am reminded of Hannibal's elephant. . . . But seriously, he added to himself, Bilibin is nothing like the figure of fun I thought he was. He may be suffering, but he's not uttering a word of complaint.

At last the worst was over. They passed the crest and saw below them very much the same view as they had seen the previous afternoon — the dry, brown Campagna stretching away to the distant shimmer of Rome.

They could still see Rome when they pitched camp that afternoon outside the walls of Monte Rotondo, with the Tiber valley at their feet.

'Are we making a circle round the dratted place?' Mark grumbled. 'Two long marches — and I can still see St. Peter's dome!'

The next morning they headed northwards, moving upstream along the bank of the Tiber. There was a new addition to the column — a score of bullocks, 'walking rations', Lorenzo called them, another of Garibaldi's good ideas from America. The beasts had been bought from peasants and paid for in hard cash. Garibaldi's rules were strict: there was to be no looting, everything was to be paid for, and the needful funds were to be borrowed from the town councils and monasteries they passed on the road, with rather slender prospects of repayment. It was very much a case of robbing the rich to pay the poor, and Mark reflected that Garibaldi resembled Robin Hood in more ways than one. On the whole, the townspeople contributed with a fair show of willingness, the monks more reluctantly.

At noon the army halted, some of the cattle were slaughtered, and soon the beef was roasting on spits over innumerable fires. It was a green, shady spot. The young Tiber came swirling down under a great stone bridge, making deep pools where, as the heat of the afternoon intensified, Mark and Lorenzo went swimming with some of the other men. Afterwards, clean and refreshed, he strolled along the bank to where Tessa was sitting under a rock, helping Anita Garibaldi to make a tent.

'This is better than yesterday,' he said contentedly.

Anita smiled. 'You found it hard? But it is my husband who should complain. What a way to spend one's birthday! Yesterday, Peppino was forty-two.'

Still, she went on, their exertions had not been wasted. All this doubling on their tracks, however wearisome and perplexing at the time, was bearing fruit. Garibaldi's hard-riding scouts, fanning out ten, twenty, even thirty miles from his line of march, were bringing back good news. They knew where the enemy were, but the enemy showed, by their movements, that they had no idea of the redshirts' whereabouts.

'Thanks to our first night-march,' she said, 'the French have sent a column chasing off to the Alban Hills. When we went east from Tivoli, we started the Spaniards on a false trail into the heart of the mountains. By now, of course, General Oudinot will have heard that we were at Monte Rotondo last night——'

'And he'll send another column after us from Rome?'

'Without doubt. But they will go in the wrong direction. Peppino will see to that. He has sent a troop of dragoons riding westwards through the country-side — they are to spread the rumour that Garibaldi is coming, that he is making for the coast to attack the French base at Civitavecchia. But in truth I think we shall now make straight northwards, with no more of this twisting and turning.'

Mark was not sure if Anita knew her husband's plans or whether, if she did, she would talk freely about them. But she did explain that there were still, in the northern part of the Papal States, some republican forces which had taken no part in the defence of Rome. If Garibaldi could unite with these troops, and raise additional regiments from among the people, the cause of Italian liberty would take on a fresh lease of life.

Mark felt considerably happier as he walked back to his companions. He realised that guerrilla warfare meant secrecy, sudden changes of plan, and the deliberate spreading of false rumours, but it was rather pleasant to be given some notion of the meaning behind it all, the eventual objective in the General's mind. There seemed room now for hope.

What was it Garibaldi had promised them? Hunger,

thirst, forced marches. . . . Well, so far, he had certainly kept his word.

There was another forced march that night, then an all-day halt at a friendly little town high in the hills. At dawn they were off again, threading their way endlessly up and down a landscape of vineyards and olive-groves and belts of forest which reminded Mark of an immense patchwork quilt. The heat was appalling. A leaden-grey haze hung over the distance, draining all colours of their brightness. The earth was dry and crumbly, the vegetation powdered with dust. There seemed to be no water anywhere. When they crossed a river their boots clattered on the loose white stones, under which there was no trickle or stain of moisture. They came to a roadside fountain: it too was dried up. At last, when the worst of the day's heat was spent, they reached a line of long horse-troughs, through which a clear runnel of water was racing from a mountain-spring.

'If Grandmother could see us now!' gasped Mark, standing back at last and wiping his sun-blistered lips.

That night they slept in an oak-wood. The next morning, which was Sunday, they came down into the plains again and entered the town of Terni to the wild cheering of the inhabitants. And not only of the inhabitants. For among the crowds pressing round them they recognized, to their delight, the uniforms of the Roman Republic.

This, evidently, was the meeting Garibaldi had planned for. For Mark and Bilibin there was another meeting which was less expected.

They had broken ranks on dismissal and were turning

away when Mark's eye was attracted by a fresh-complexioned boy of about his own age standing among the townspeople. He murmured a comment to Bilibin, who — following his usual principle that, although all foreigners ought to understand English perfectly, none of them in fact knew a word — answered cheerfully: 'Yes, remarkable! With a face like that he almost could *be* British!'

To Mark's horror the young stranger grinned broadly, but before either of them could speak there came a crisp voice from behind which made Bilibin spin round like a teetotum.

'He not only could be British, sir, but he *is* British. That boy, sir, is my son, sir. And may I ask, who the devil are you, sir?'

No one, at least, could have doubted the speaker's nationality. With his elegantly-tailored summer suit, his spotless white chimney-pot hat, he could only be an English gentleman travelling on the Continent. Bilibin flinched for a moment under those steely eyes, then drew himself up and answered with a firmness which (Mark felt sure) he could never have mustered in the old days: 'My name is Bilibin, sir. Jonathan Bilibin. And I am a clerk in Holy Orders.'

'Well, I'll be hanged! I'm Forbes, Colonel Forbes. Late of the Coldstream Guards.'

Chapter Thirteen

THE CLOSING NET

'My pater says the Tuscans will be no use at all. If Garibaldi expects any help in that quarter, he's in for a disappointment. And my pater knows.' Hugh Forbes spoke with airy assurance. He had caught something of his father's manner. Mark was not quite sure how well the two of them would get on but it was certainly a pleasant change, that first evening, to talk to an English boy. They sat at a trestle-table outside an inn, a little apart from Bilibin and the Colonel.

The Colonel, it seemed, was the commander of those other Republican forces with which Garibaldi had now united. He was a wealthy man who had lived in Tuscany for years. 'My stepmother,' the boy explained, 'is partly Italian.' The Colonel had become interested in the cause of Italian unity. 'Interested' was a typical Forbes understatement. Within the past eighteen months he had fought for the Venetians against the Austrians and for the Sicilians against Bomba. When that revolt was quenched, he had made his way to the northern territories of the Roman Republic and had another go at the Austrians. Now his troops were reduced to less than a thousand — and his son was not complimentary about their quality.

'Terrible scallywags, a lot of them. Steal anything!'

'Not all of ours are angels,' Mark admitted, 'but Garibaldi won't have thieving, and they know it. They say that, if a soldier steals, Garibaldi will order him to be hanged without a moment's hesitation — without even taking his cigar out of his mouth! I don't know if he's ever really done it. But the men believe it, and that's the main thing.'

'If the pater hanged his thieves, he'd have no men left. All he can do is make them wear their coats inside out, as a mark of disgrace.'

It was all rather depressing. Everyone had set such hopes on this arrival at Terni. They were to have linked up with another army — which had now dwindled to a mere nine hundred unwilling warriors. They were then to have invaded Tuscany and called on the Tuscan people to throw out their Austrian Grand Duke for the second time. Tuscany was to have taken up the fight for Italy, now that Rome was temporarily knocked out of it.

According to young Forbes, however, the Tuscans could be relied upon for nothing but talk. And so, in the next few days, it proved.

When the combined army left Terni, so many deserters had slipped away that they offset the Colonel's contingent and Garibaldi commanded no more men than before. Nor did fresh volunteers flock to his standard. And when, as expected, they pushed forward into Tuscany, and Garibaldi issued a manifesto calling on the inhabitants to rise against the Austrians, his appeal fell flat.

'What now?' Mark asked dejectedly.

'There's only one thing, I should say,' said Forbes.

'Cross the Apennines to the Adriatic — seize a port and some shipping — and sail to Venice. That's what Garibaldi's discussing with my pater. Venice is still holding out. Incredible, really. If we could get to Venice we might tip the scale there.'

'That would be wonderful,' said Tessa wistfully. She herself did not complain of the hard campaigning life, but these endless marches were bad for Anita. Venice would be better, even a Venice beleaguered by the Austrians. At least there would be rest, shelter, and proper medical attention. 'And it would be near Verona,' she added. Since Pietro's death, Mark knew, she had clung more and more to the idea of her native city, the city she could not remember but had dreamed of all her childhood, Verona with its racing river of grey-green Alpine water, its old bridge with the swallow-tailed battlements, its cypress-studded hills.

'Odd girl, that,' said Forbes when she left them. 'I suppose she could be quite a good-looker — in an Italian way — if she hadn't hacked her hair off and dressed up in trousers.'

'She *is*.'

'My stepmother is considered *really* beautiful. She stayed behind in Siena. My pater doesn't approve of women getting mixed up with this sort of thing.'

'Tessa hasn't a lot of choice,' said Mark stiffly, but he was privately relieved at the other boy's indifferent tone. Tessa, he was well aware, had been impressed by his confident manner, his fluent Italian, his immaculate linen suits. By comparison he himself looked, he well knew, like a November guy.

'Your Mr. Bilibin's a queer fish too.'

Mark could not deny it. Two days ago, when Garibaldi had been issuing his appeal to the Tuscan people and everybody had been hoping against hope for some miraculous result, Bilibin had been absorbed in the distant view of Lake Trasimene. He had gone on and on about Hannibal's annihilation of the ancient Romans when the others were far more concerned about their own probable annihilation by the French and Austrians.

'Still,' went on Forbes, 'he seems to get on all right with my pater — which I wouldn't have expected. Perhaps it's because they are both old Oxford men.'

There was nothing left now but to cross the great chain of the Apennines and make for the east coast. The dream of raising Central Italy in revolt was abandoned. It was a question of escape. They had to face it: they had become fugitives.

It was cruelly brought home to them when they reached Arezzo and found the gates barred. The anti-democratic party controlled the town. They had armed the local peasants. There were also a few Tuscan and Austrian troops inside.

There was a miserable day of wrangling, while Garibaldi tried to arrange a peaceful entry. Some of the men clamoured to attack the place. Garibaldi said no, Italians must not fight Italians, Arezzo was a patriotic town. . . . If it had not sent so many volunteers to fight for Italy elsewhere, it would not now be in the hands of the opposition. Also, there was no time to fight their way into a town which did not receive them willingly.

o   199

Two Austrian armies were now hard on their heels, one from Florence and one from Perugia. They must hurry on into the mountains.

So they passed Arezzo disdainfully by. As it was, the rearguard was overtaken by the Austrians and severely mauled. When the survivors made contact again with the main body, they brought grim stories of wounded men and stragglers murdered by hostile peasants. It was a bitter thought.

'We expect to die for Italy,' said Lorenzo passionately, 'but not this way!'

They had long ago abandoned the waggons and transferred their supplies to pack-mules, but the one little cannon was still painfully dragged on, up hill and down dale, more as a symbol of determination than for its military value. Garibaldi rode in front with Anita and his staff. Tessa was usually with them, but sometimes she dropped back and kept pace with Mark and Bilibin, offering her horse for spells to any man who was finding it hard to keep up.

Behind the leaders came the last handful of Masina's lancers with their red fezzes and tattered fluttering pennants. Then the dark string of pack-mules, followed by a milk-white herd of cattle, lowing deeply and tossing their long-horned heads under the onslaught of the flies. . . . After these, the redshirts with their sun-blackened faces. . . . Finally the Colonel and his son, with their own contingent and the Lombards in their sombre rifle-green.

It was a small army now, thought Mark, looking forward and back as they wound their painful way up into the hills. It had lost weight, like the footsore half-starved individuals who composed it. Perhaps it was a healthy loss — as it certainly was in the case of Bilibin, who had now no trace of flabbiness and (though he would never look like a skeleton) had fined down to an almost athletic figure. So too the army as a whole had lost its moral flabbiness. The criminal element had made themselves scarce, the faint-hearted had deserted and slipped away to their homes, it was mostly the dedicated patriots who remained. And, of course, the odd fish like himself, Bilibin, the fire-eating Colonel and his son.

More than once he tried to apologize to the curate for dragging him into such hardships and dangers. Bilibin waved away his regrets.

'The journey is full of unexpected compensations. It has deepened my understanding in all kinds of ways. For example, the next time I read Xenophon, I shall be much better able to picture the Retreat of the Ten Thousand.'

'If there were ten thousand of us,' said Mark wryly, 'it wouldn't need to be a retreat.'

They crossed the Scopettone Pass and threaded their way down the long gorge beside the Cerfone, till they saw the wide vine-carpeted valley of the upper Tiber in front of them. Here, in the hilltop village of Citerna, Garibaldi gave them a much-needed breathing-space. Citerna, with its ruined castle-keep and white-walled monasteries, was remote as an eagle's nest. They looked down over dizzy slopes of shimmering grey olive-trees to the green valley-floor stretching away for miles. East-wards, across the poplar-lined young river, rose the main mass of the Apennines. They could see the faint streak of the road they would have to climb to cross it and reach the Adriatic.

They spent two days at Citerna, camped in the monastery grounds. Anita and Tessa pitched their tent in a thicket of shady evergreens. Anita knew that her husband never liked his men to scatter in billets among the houses and she was so used to the cowboy life herself that she had no wish to sleep indoors. Tessa never tired of listening to the story of her South American adventures and Mark's friendship with Tessa gave him frequent opportunities to join the audience. As Colonel Forbes was in constant consultation with Garibaldi, Hugh also was seldom far away.

It was evening when they first saw the Austrians.

Mark had noticed the staff officers move hurriedly across the grounds and take up their position on the wall. It was obvious that they were watching something of great interest in the valley below. Soon more and more soldiers drifted over to see. Mark and his friends joined the crowd lining the parapet.

'Just look at them!' said Hugh Forbes.

The whitecoats were creeping about like ants. In that vast landscape they could be distinguished as three separate armies. Mark overheard the Colonel say:

'They obviously can't see each other. I doubt if they know of each other's whereabouts. Their information is always very poor, they seem to have no notion of co-operating.'

It would have been funny, looking down upon those

blindly groping columns so far below them, if it had not been necessary to cross that same valley before reaching the mountains again.

'I expect,' said Mark, 'we shall do one of our famous night-marches.'

'H'm,' said Forbes, 'my pater says a night-march is a mighty tricky operation, even with properly disciplined troops.'

'Don't worry. It's Garibaldi's favourite amusement.'

Mark tried to sound confident but he realised that a night-march in this case would be a very different proposition from those in which he had so far taken part. The Austrians, however imperfect their communications, knew that Garibaldi was in the neighbourhood and had not yet crossed the upper Tiber. They were waiting for him down there. He wondered how the General was going to deal with this problem.

Nor did the outlook brighten as time went by. The next morning Hugh Forbes, full of the latest information from his father, painted a sombre picture.

'They obviously know we're up here. My pater says they're planting batteries to shell the village. But if we cut and run for it, the other whitecoats are blocking every road out of the valley. The only one that seems to be unguarded is the one we want, over the Bocca Trabaria. My pater says he can only suppose that it isn't marked on their maps and they can't see the road itself from down there.'

'That's all right then.'

'We've still got to reach it, Apperley.'

'We shall.'

With the nearest of the Austrian divisions closing in upon Citerna it was time to move if they were not to be trapped on that isolated summit. So, that evening, Garibaldi put his plan into operation. It was more complicated than usual — as the complicated circumstances required. One detachment made a feint attack against the whitecoats during the afternoon, another stayed behind on the hill as long as possible to deceive the enemy, and the main body set off, silent as usual, at dusk, to cross the valley in two columns by two different routes. The monks of Citerna, much against their will, accompanied Mark's own column for a number of miles and had to splash knee-deep, their habits lifted high, through the sandy fords of the Tiber. Garibaldi dared not risk leaving them behind lest they sent word of his movements to the Austrians.

Mark had to agree that a night-march *was* a 'mighty tricky operation' and that his earlier experiences near Rome had been child's play by comparison. This time, instead of a well-trodden road, there were narrow paths through dark vineyards and olive-groves, the route was confused with winding streams, and instead of a single column there were several, which somehow had to be reunited at one time and place. A lot of equipment was lost or abandoned. Quite a number of men got detached from their party and were not seen again. They dropped further and further behind, stumbling about in the blackness of the night.

'God help them if the whitecoats catch them,' said Bellotti. 'It will be the firing squad — or a flogging at the least. They are great floggers, the *tedeschi.*'

Mark shivered and made up his mind never, under any circumstances, to wander away from the column.

At dawn, exhausted but triumphant, they reached San Giustino at the foot of the pass, and after a few hours' rest began the gruelling zigzag climb. Looking back, Mark saw the whitecoat formations still weaving their pointless patterns on the green carpet of the valley.

Garibaldi had done it again.

But these two thousand men were fighting an empire, an empire which sprawled across Europe from Bohemia and Poland down into the Balkans, and could match every band of rebels with an army corps. They had outflanked, outmarched and outwitted the divisions hunting them on the western side of the Apennines, but when, after a few hours' sleep on the highest part of the pass, they made their way down the eastern valleys, it was only to find two fresh Austrian columns converging upon them.

The next two days were bad. Garibaldi, with his usual flair, found a by-road unknown to the enemy and managed to slip by — if 'slip' was a proper word to describe their painful, dogged trudging through that inhospitable countryside. It was impossible to throw the enemy off the scent. Though the Austrians could not overtake the redshirts and bring them to battle, their Tyrolese riflemen managed to keep up a running duel with the Bersaglieri, who formed the rearguard under the imperturbable Colonel Forbes. There were ferocious Hungarian hussars, too, who had trailed the fugitives all the way from the Tiber valley and pounced like vultures on any who straggled behind.

It was a bleak, sun-blistered landscape, the hills scoured and eroded, brown and grey, the valley-floors all loose stones, polished white and clattering underfoot, with nowhere a trickle of water.

Mark said to Bilibin: 'I don't see how *this* army is going to capture a seaport. Not with the Austrians everywhere.'

'No.' Bilibin hesitated. 'I have been talking to the Colonel. I — I like to look ahead.'

'Yes?' Mark spoke warily. Bilibin had not mentioned Grandmother for days — they had had more pressing fears — but he knew that the curate had never lost sight of his original responsibility.

'I think that even Garibaldi now sees the hopelessness of trying to reach Venice. The present idea is to make for San Marino and ask for sanctuary. You will recollect, Mark, San Marino is an independent republic — quite tiny, but independent, and therefore neutral?'

'I've heard of it, sir. What'll happen then?'

'Garibaldi and his men will be granted political asylum — provided of course that they lay down their arms — and the Austrians will not be able to touch them. We, as British subjects, should have no great difficulty, the Colonel thinks. Once all the details are settled, we shall be issued with passes and be able to make our way home unmolested.'

'It seems a miserable end to it all.' Mark turned his head away, his eyes pricking with sudden angry tears.

'Can you see any better end to it?' asked Bilibin gently. But for a few moments Mark could see nothing at all.

At sunrise on the last day of July, four unforgettable weeks after they had left Rome, they saw the battlements of San Marino blackly silhouetted on their crag, hundreds of feet sheer above the surrounding countryside. No sight was ever more welcome. Ugo Bassi had ridden ahead the previous day to inquire if the miniature republic would risk Austrian displeasure by giving them refuge and in the middle of the night he had sent back an urgent message. Yes, San Marino would admit the fugitives if they would lay down their arms, but unless they came at once it would be too late. From the top of that crag the friar had seen the distant camp-fires of yet another Austrian army, about which Garibaldi knew nothing. Garibaldi must hurry forward and get his men across the border or this last escape-route would be cut.

So, as the sunshine gathered strength on the rocky slopes of Monte Tassona, the scarecrow army struggled forward across the last few miles. The actual border was marked by a steep ravine, beyond which the road spiralled, through safe neutral territory, to the town of San Marino high above. Here, in the last few yards, the little cannon stuck and refused to budge, as though unwilling to give up the struggle for Italy. A crowd of redshirts bunched round it, Mark among them, and an excited debate developed.

'Leave it——'

'Never! After coming so far with us?'

'What does it matter — now? We shall have to give it up when we're interned.'

'That's not the same as leaving it to the cursed white-coats!'

'If we could get hold of some oxen——'

'We want a stout pole to act as a lever——'

It was laughable, thought Mark, how all these men forgot their weariness and despair when faced with the interesting practical problem of getting the cannon up the side of the ravine.

Various suggestions were tried, with interruptions from those who saw no sense in bothering at this stage. No one realised how much time had been wasted until suddenly bullets began to fly and turning their heads they saw white uniforms against the brown rocks behind them. There was a period of confusion. Some of the legionaries and Bersaglieri knelt and fired back, others (who had already argued that the war was over, and who saw no point in getting killed in the last minute) went scrambling up the hill on the neutral side. Mark was just reloading when, to his horror, he heard Anita's voice and saw her not ten yards away, sitting her horse amid the hail of shots.

'Where is Peppino?'

'He's in the town, Signora! He went on ahead — he didn't know about the Austrians——'

'Why are these men running away?' Her scorn was terrible. She broke into a flood of strident abuse. Many of the fugitives turned, ashamed, and fired back at the Austrians. The Colonel appeared, top-hatted as always, as self-possessed as though he were in the Royal Enclosure at Ascot but rallying the men with language which would scarcely have been appropriate there. The Austrian advance came to a halt. By the time Garibaldi came thundering down the hill to take charge again, the brief panic was forgotten. On the very threshold of safety the fugitives turned at bay and defied their pursuers.

Garibaldi looked down at the cannon, then shrugged his shoulders in resignation. It was stuck there at the bottom of the ravine and was worth no man's life. He was never one for useless sentiment. He gave the order to move on. Covered to the last by the rifles of the rearguard, the column began to wend its way up the hill.

'Thank God,' muttered Bilibin fervently, 'it is all over.'

In that, as in many other things, poor Bilibin was much mistaken.

Chapter Fourteen

THE WAY TO VENICE

'THIS looks like the end of the road,' said Forbes
with a yawn.

They had slept all afternoon in the grounds of
the Capuchin monastery outside the town-gates. It was
strange to wake up and to realise that no bugle would
blow for the resumption of the march. There was no
distant gunfire, there were no white-uniformed pursuers.
Instead, there were gentle-voiced friars in brown habits
with long pointed hoods, showing them where they
could wash, where the wounded were lying, cleanly
bandaged and comfortable, and where the kindly citizens
of San Marino had stacked gifts of wine and provisions
for the refugees.

'Yes, the end of the road,' Mark agreed sadly.

One could be grateful for everything and yet feel bitter
that it had all ended like this. He leant his elbows on the
garden-wall and stared across twelve miles of coastal

plain to where the Adriatic stretched pale but clear in the hard brilliance of evening.

'So near and yet so far . . .'

'Yes.'

Mark thought of the Greeks in that famous passage of Xenophon. *'Thalassa! Thalassa!'* they had cried exultantly, 'The sea! The sea!', when, after their tortuous retreat through the mountains of Asia Minor, they had sighted the Black Sea. But for them there had been an important difference: the Ten Thousand had been free to press forward to the coast and take ship for home. There was no such happy climax for Garibaldi's volunteers. The sea mocked them like a mirage. They could get no nearer to it because of the Austrians.

For the third time the boys re-read the paper which fluttered on a near-by door. It was the epitaph of the adventure, the death-certificate of all their hopes. It ran:

'*REPUBLIC OF SAN MARINO*
Order of the Day, July 31, 1849, 2 p.m.
Soldiers!
We have reached sanctuary and owe the best behaviour towards our generous hosts. We ourselves deserve consideration for the misfortunes which have pursued us.

As from this moment I release my companions from all obligation. I leave you at liberty to return to private life. But remember that Italy must not continue in shame, and that it is better to die than to live as slaves of the foreigner.
GARIBALDI.'

'Ah, here you are!'

Tessa spoke behind them. She had changed into a skirt, she was washed and tidied, but she did not look as though she had slept much.

'How are things?' asked Mark.

'She is far from well——'

'The Signora?'

'Yes. I am worried about her. I hope she will be all right now we have got here. She will sleep in a proper bed tonight. All the people here are so kind to us.'

'What's the General doing?'

'Oh, there is a meeting. They are discussing terms. Everything has to be agreed with the Austrians — and we have to be sure that they will keep their word. Myself,' said Tessa, her earrings shaking with much of her old spirit, 'I would not trust them a yard! But we shall see.'

'We haven't a lot of choice,' said young Forbes.

Nor had they. They were marooned on an islet of neutral territory, surrounded by a sea of enemies. San Marino was no more than a few square miles of rugged mountain, thrusting two or three thousand feet up into the air, with a single road for exit — and no coastline of her own. Her generous inhabitants could not for ever feed their uninvited guests, yet, unless they grew wings, they could never leave without walking into the arms of the Austrians.

So the evening passed and the refugees waited anxiously to hear what terms would be arranged. The sunset died in orange glory behind the ink-black Apennines. Mark remembered bygone sunsets seen from the ridge of the Malverns, when the Welsh mountains had similarly stood out against the western blaze. One always felt a little natural sadness at the dying of the day, but never more so than now, when something else was passing too. Evening spread green wings across the eastern sky. A chill breeze played round the high-perched town. Miles away, in the shadowed plain, the Austrian camp-fires began to twinkle redly, one after another, like the gathering of a wolf-pack.

Most of the volunteers settled down for the night. Mark did not feel like sleep. He was not, like so many of his elders, drowsy and relaxed with wine. He sat in a sheltered corner with Bilibin, discussing in low tones every subject under the sun. Then, anxious to learn if anything had yet been decided, they strolled through the gates to the café which Garibaldi was using as headquarters.

They could see the General sitting over the remains of a late supper. The Colonel, Ugo Bassi and several other officers were there. So was Anita. Tessa sat by herself, apart. She saw Mark and Bilibin through the open doorway and came out to them.

'You look exhausted, my dear,' said Bilibin. 'You should be asleep.'

She shook her head. 'I shall wait for the Signora.' She glanced back into the café, then continued in a low voice: 'Besides, I have a strange feeling that something is going to happen.'

'Happen?'

'I heard him say the Austrian terms were "unacceptable".'

'Do you know what they are?' Mark whispered.

'We are to hand over our arms to the Captains Regent of San Marino, *they* will pass them to the Austrians, and the Austrians will let us go home. They say!' She sounded dubious. 'The General and his wife must go back to America.'

'Is he going to refuse? What else can he do?'

'Who knows — with Garibaldi? He was talking a long time with the Signora. He was begging her to do something. She kept shaking her head. I heard her say, "You want to leave me", and after that he did not try to persuade her any more.'

Mark looked at Bilibin. 'It sounds as if he has some plan . . .'

'They kept mentioning Venice,' said Tessa.

'But Venice is now out of the question,' said Bilibin.

'I do not know, Mr. Bilibin. Something is going to happen — that I am sure. But it is being kept secret. It must be hidden even from the people of San Marino.'

'In that case it'll have to be hidden from us,' Mark grumbled. 'If the whole army knew, it'd be certain to leak out in the town. Still, most of the fellows have turned in for the night now, so I suppose it makes no difference.'

'I think we too should turn in, dear boy.'

'Oh, no, sir — not while Tessa has to hang about.'

'Tessa should certainly go to bed.'

'I wait for the Signora. I go when she goes,' said the girl firmly. 'And *where*,' she added.

Three peasants appeared from the darkness and stood hesitating in the lighted doorway. Then Garibaldi came out to them, his cigar glowing furiously, his map open in his hand. He sat down, the peasants grouped round him, and there was a long discussion in undertones. The friends moved politely to a little distance. The conference was joined by Colonel Forbes and the other staff officers. Anita Garibaldi came out behind them.

'Tessa! I thought you were asleep hours ago!'

'I am waiting for you, *signora*.'

'I . . . I shall be a little while. Go. Good night——' She put her arms impulsively round Tessa and kissed her. 'God bless you. And thank you for everything.'

'I shall wait, *signora*.'

Anita made no answer. She gave Tessa a long look and turned away. The atmosphere had suddenly become charged with tension. A little crowd of soldiers who were still awake began to gather in the gloom beyond the circle of lantern-light. There was the sound of horses being led across the flagstones at a slow walk. Mark recognized the General's white charger, Anita's own horse, the friar's English thoroughbred . . . Whether by misunderstanding, or because he was meant for someone else to ride, even Tessa's sturdy little bay gelding had been brought round too.

Garibaldi stood up and threw away the butt of his cigar. He looked round and raised his voice just sufficiently for them all to hear.

'Whoever wants to follow me, I offer only more battles, hardships and exile. But pacts with the foreigner, never!'

It was extraordinary. The choice was thrown at them for instant decision. Garibaldi was in the saddle, so were Anita and the officers . . . They were moving towards the gateway when someone remembered that Ugo Bassi was still in the café, quietly absorbed in writing. They fetched him out and he mounted. There was no time for discussion. Neither the town nor the rest of the refugees must be roused, or no one at all would get away. There was just time to run for one's own arms and equipment, if one wished to go, and then to follow, once more, the black plume that tossed for a moment in the lantern-light and then went bobbing away into the darkness down the mountainside.

Tessa never hesitated. She ran forward and claimed her gelding, hitched up her skirt, and scrambled astride. Mark saw that argument was impossible and hurried off for his musket and knapsack. Bilibin came stumbling at his heels.

Seeing a paler shape among the others, Mark mistook it for Hugh Forbes in his light fawn suit — and had his head nearly bitten off for his pains.

'Quiet, you young fool!' said the Colonel. 'Keep your voice down.'

Mark apologized so discreetly as to be almost inaudible. The Colonel relented somewhat.

'I left my boy asleep,' he whispered.

'Then——'

'He'll be all right. Safer there than here. He's done enough. Same applies to you. Anyhow, no chance to get hold of him.'

A strange pair, thought Mark . . . But the Colonel was logical. He had had to choose quickly. He had put Italy first. No doubt he was right: his son, and all the others left sleeping round the gates of San Marino, would be better off where they were.

There was no more whispering after that. They stole down the road like thieves. Mark had no idea how many men were in front of them. He knew that he and Bilibin were among the last. Ugo Bassi was just behind. The Colonel had dropped into his usual place as commander of the rearguard.

At the bottom of the mountain they came to an almost dry river-bed, a vast expanse of bone-white stones and silvery sand, which glimmered spectrally before them. They must be out of San Marino now. Silence was doubly vital, doubly difficult, for the smooth stones slipped and clinked underfoot and there were lingering pools of water where least expected. It must have been a quarter of a mile from bank to bank and their devious route made it seem endless. They were filing up the opposite side when a guttural voice challenged them.

There was no hope of concealment now. Rifles cracked, the wall of darkness flashed and sputtered with flame, bullets screeched shrilly across the boulders, there was a trampling of horsemen along the bank . . .

'Steady!' said the Colonel. 'Keep together. We must gain time for the others in front.'

They stood their ground, blazing away at dim shapes sweeping round them. There were not many of the enemy. They seemed to be only a cavalry patrol and they did not press their attack. They could not know the strength of the Italians. Still less could they know that these were the last and not the first of the column.

'Come on,' grunted the Colonel. 'Mustn't lose contact.'

He led them forward at a brisk run. A few yards brought them to the comparative safety of another steep mountainside. They could hear their friends high above them and there was just enough light to see the mule-track in front of their feet. They went scuttling up. A few carbines banged at them in futile fashion from below, but the Austrians showed no desire to risk their necks in pursuit.

'We're through,' said the Colonel cheerfully. 'That river was the Marecchia. We knew there were white-coats both upstream and down — the guide reckoned we could just about slip between them.'

They pressed on at full pelt over paths that seemed hardly paths at all. But, the Colonel assured them, Garibaldi had found the best guide in San Marino and he knew what he was doing. Sunrise brought them to a friendly village, where they collapsed at the roadside and the people came crowding out to them with bottles of wine, crisp new bread, and delicious water-melons. It was possible now to look round and see who was there. Mark guessed that there were now only two or three hundred men in the column.

No hope today of a long siesta to make up for one night-march and prepare for the next! They must go forward again at top speed. There must be no stopping before they reached some suitable point on the coast unguarded by the enemy.

So, through the morning and the ever-hotter afternoon, they struggled on over that crumpled landscape of hill and valley until at last the flat plain opened at their feet, stretching away to the sea.

'That river,' said the Colonel, 'is the Rubicon. The little town beyond, on the coast, is Cesenatico. That's where we're making for. But first we must cross the Rubicon.'

Bilibin, weary though he was, could not help saying that Caesar, of course, crossed it in the opposite direction. In 49 B.C. Nobody contradicted Bilibin.

It took them another six hours to cross the plain. Darkness had long fallen when they saw the lights of the little fishing-port glimmering ahead of them.

They had been on the road for twenty-two hours since leaving San Marino.

Cesenatico seemed to consist mainly of a piazza and a broad main street, with a canal running down its centre to the harbour. A few lanterns cast wobbling yellow reflections in the glassy water and picked out, against the pale back-cloth of the houses, the hard black outline of masts and rigging. Here were the hoped-for fishing-boats, about a dozen of them, moored at their owners' doors after the day's work.

Most of the townspeople had gone to bed. A handful of Austrian soldiers were playing cards in the guardhouse, so absorbed in their game that Garibaldi and his mounted companions had swept into the middle of the town before any alarm was raised. When Mark arrived a few minutes later it was all over, and a quaking cluster of prisoners, Papal Carabineers as well as Austrians, had been rounded up in the piazza to hear their fate.

'Shoot them!' cried a harsh voice. 'They'll only give us away, afterwards.'

Several other voices called out in agreement. Men remembered bitterly what had been done to their friends who had fallen by the wayside in the retreat.

'No, no,' protested Ugo Bassi.

'The officer, then! The Carabineer! He's a traitor to Italy!'

'No,' said Garibaldi. 'That's what the whitecoats would do. We are not going to imitate their methods.'

'But they'll give the alarm, the minute we've gone!'

'Then we must take them with us.' Garibaldi turned to Colonel Forbes. 'Will you cover our rear as usual, Colonel? We will take care of these prisoners, but we cannot guarantee that no one else will slip out of the town and take word to the Austrians. Will you make sure that no one leaves until we are ready to start?'

'Certainly, sir.'

Mark and Bilibin returned with the Colonel's little party to the last of the houses straggling back along the road inland. Detachments were sent to bar every other route. Barricades were built of farm-carts and furniture. Not content with posting sentries at every barricade, the Colonel placed a couple of men in ambush a little distance along the road, so that if any informer managed to avoid the visible road-blocks, he would be caught at the very moment when he felt out of danger.

So midnight came and passed. Mark dozed off once for a little while, sprawled out on the hard ground with those others who were not on guard. Mostly, though, despite their exhaustion, they were too tense for sleep.

There was no certainty that the Austrians would not learn, even without a message from the town itself, that Garibaldi had reached Cesenatico. At any minute the rising moon might reveal a squadron of hussars coming down the road.

What was happening at the harbour? What on earth was Garibaldi *doing*? All was quiet now. There had been plenty of noise in the first hour — a great banging on doors and a tumult of shrill argument which had carried for hundreds of yards to the impatient listeners at the barricades — but now it was almost as though the towns-people, and for that matter the redshirts, had retired for the night.

Colonel Forbes stalked up and down in his top-hat, bending his ramrod spine only to squint tetchily at his watch in the dim light of a lantern.

'This is the devil,' he muttered in English. 'We *must* get to sea by daylight, or it's all up. Apperley!'

'Sir?'

'Run along and see what's holding them up. Don't say anything, mind. If the General spots you and asks, you can say that the situation is well in hand. I'll take my oath no one has slipped through the cordon. But that doesn't mean that these confounded Austrians mayn't turn up just the same. He knows that as well as I do.'

'Very good, sir.'

Mark hurried back into the town as fast as his aching legs would carry him. The boats had vanished from their moorings. He had to walk half a mile down the canal until he found them, bunched in the harbour-mouth, which was made by two stone-and-timber moles built out into the shallow sea. Fishermen and redshirts were standing around in groups, some arguing furiously, others moodily silent. Mark saw Anita sitting on the quay, propped up against some sacks. The horses were tethered close by. Tessa turned as he called her name.

'Marco!'

'Can you tell me what's happening? It'll soon be dawn. We've been here for hours.'

'I know. It is terrible. First we had to rouse all these fishermen. Some of them do not want to help us. They are afraid for their boats, they are afraid of what the Austrians will do to them afterwards.'

'I can understand that,' said Mark grimly.

'However, they came. And then there was the mayor and the council. There were many things which Garibaldi demanded — food and so forth — and new gear had to be found for some of the boats. And now, to cap everything, the fishermen say they cannot put to sea! There has been a squall, the breakers are very bad, it is impossible to sail out against them.'

'In that case it's about the finish, then. The Austrians will be here in the morning. If we can't get away by sea, we certainly can't get away by land.'

'Garibaldi will think of something, I am sure. And now I must go back to the Signora. She is feeling very ill after the long day.'

Mark was not anxious to go straight back to the Colonel with such depressing news. Seeing Garibaldi and the officers a little further along the quay, deep in discussion with some of the skippers, he edged near them in the hope of hearing something better. One of the fishermen was saying, with eloquent gestures:

'I swear to you, General, in a sea like this it is utterly impossible.'

'Impossible?' Garibaldi growled like a cornered lion. 'You say this to me? To me — a master mariner? If you cannot get your boats out of this harbour, I will.'

'Forgive me, General — but we know our own harbour, my neighbours and I, we know this coast, and you do not. I do not see how——'

'I will show you how! If we cannot sail them out, we can warp them out. Come on! I want a small boat and some men who can row well. I want a couple of kedge-anchors lashed together. I want cables. Look lively! And don't tell me you don't understand or you can't do it. I know as much about the sea as you!'

There was muttering, but no more contradiction. Men went busily to work, spurred on by Garibaldi's sharp tongue and sometimes even by the whack of a flat sword. Mark stayed to watch the operation, fascinated by its difficulty, excusing himself with the thought that there was no sense in going back to the Colonel until there was some success to report. As the moonlight changed by degrees into the glimmer of dawn, he stood on the end of one jetty and watched the struggle with the surf outside the harbour-mouth.

Garibaldi himself went out in the little boat which was to drop the anchors. The men at the oars battled manfully, but time after time the curling breakers threw them back. Finally, with one or two helpers, he went over the side into the turbulent shallows and, with the water foaming round his shoulders, helped to thrust the craft those critical few yards forward into the open sea. For some minutes Mark saw him swimming about, making fast the anchors. Then, to everyone's delight, the boat turned for home, paying out cables foot by foot. Mark was starting back with this good news when a chorus of groans made him turn his head. A weak cable had parted, a new one had to be found, everything must be done again.

Still, he was confident now that Garibaldi would do it — if only the weather grew no worse and the Austrians did not arrive. He hurried back to the Colonel and explained what was happening.

'H'm. It's going to be a deuced near thing.' The Colonel could read his watch in the strengthening daylight. 'Half past five,' he grunted.

It was another half-hour before a messenger came riding back from the harbour. The boats were being warped out successfully now. The first of them were clear of the harbour-mouth, had cast off their helpful cables, and were standing out to sea. The Colonel's covering party was to fall slowly back in sections. The last boats would wait until everyone had embarked.

'Excellent! Mr. Bilibin——'

'Yes, Colonel?'

'As a non-combatant you had better go with the first section. The boy will go with you.'

'Sir——' Mark began.

'Don't argue,' said the Colonel. 'Obey orders.'

For the third and last time Mark trudged wearily down that endless village-street beside the canal. Nearly all the boats had gone. They looked like patterned butterflies as they stood out into the milky Adriatic, unfurling their lateen sails of red and saffron-yellow, sepia and white and tangerine. Only two boats remained alongside the quay, each gaily-painted bow with its carved figurehead of some nymph or goddess blowing a trumpet to the sky. Tessa was helping Anita aboard. Garibaldi was giving his white charger a final pat as he handed the reins to one of the townsmen. Suddenly he kissed the horse on the forehead and, as he turned away, Mark heard him say gruffly: 'Do what you like with him — but never let the Austrians get hold of him!' Then, raising his voice to the other men standing round, he said something which Mark had heard him say more than once during those last few days: *'Good-bye. Within ten years I shall be back.'*

'Come on,' Tessa called. 'There is room with us, Mr. Bilibin!'

They followed Garibaldi into the boat. A few minutes of hauling on the cable brought them safely through the flurry of surf at the end of the pier. Glancing back, Mark was relieved to see the white top-hat moving with slow dignity along the last few yards to the remaining boat. Of the Austrians there was still no sign.

'All aboard for Venice!' he murmured happily to Tessa.

Chapter Fifteen

'ILL MET BY MOONLIGHT'

THE sun came up into a cloudless sky. It would have been pitiless, beating down upon them, if they had been marching still through the unshaded hills. But now they could stretch out in the blessed shadow of the sail, while a favouring breeze, cool off the water, sped them effortlessly northwards to Venice.

When they got there, fresh troubles and hardships would be waiting. All knew that. The news from the besieged city was not good: the Austrians tightening their ring, food supplies dwindling, typhus and cholera rampant in the overcrowded courts and alleys. These things must be faced tomorrow or the next day, not now. Mark was not the only one who spent most of that long August day sprawled in the deep sleep of utter exhaustion. It was evening when he became conscious of his surroundings.

'Water . . . water . . .'

It was the low moan of a woman's voice he heard. He sat up and blinked. In the stern he could see Anita Garibaldi reclining on a mattress. Her husband and Ugo Bassi were crouching beside her. She seemed delirious.

Tessa was sitting hunched on a thwart near by. Mark stretched out his hand and touched her sleeve. She looked round, her eyes moist.

'Ah, Marco! You feel better?'

'Much. What about you?'

'Oh, I am all right. It is the Signora. It is terrible. Always she cries out for water. And we have scarcely any water. There was a muddle over provisioning the boats. It is the same with the others.' She nodded towards the rest of the little flotilla strung out across the sea. 'We have asked those we could get near. They are all short.'

'Is she very bad, Tessa?'

'I am afraid for her. She should have stayed at San Marino. Indeed, she should never have come on the march from Rome at all. But — what's the use? She and Garibaldi are a pair. A law to themselves, never afraid. And because they are a pair, they will not be divided.'

'I hate to hear her moaning like that.'

'I too. She would not make a murmur if she were not in a fever. She does not know where she is.'

'Perhaps she will be better when the sun goes down. It will be cooler, she may not feel so thirsty.'

'I hope so. I can only pray.'

Sunset came. The coast became a long line, black, low, and edged with gold and fire. It was the first time since arriving in Italy that Mark had been out of sight of hills. The coastal plain was widening into the land of lagoons and marshes which stretched more or less continuously to Venice.

A beautiful evening followed the beautiful day. The moon was nearing its full. It flooded sea and land with a serene silvery radiance. Each boat stood out clearly, its sail a dark wing on the mirror-like sheen of the water. Miles away, the level shore was a black ribbon edging the velvet of the night sky.

But all that beauty brought its own doom. The very clarity of the moonlight betrayed them. Towards ten o'clock a shout from one of the legionaries brought Garibaldi scrambling into the bows.

'The devil!' he muttered. 'Our luck is out.'

Far out to sea, but creeping across to intercept them, were fresh sails, and these were white under the moon. They had escaped from the Austrian army only to run into the navy.

' "*Ill met by moonlight*," ' Bilibin quoted grimly.

Now Mark saw Garibaldi as the seaman, roaring quick decisive orders at the crew. The fishermen obeyed sullenly. Every stitch of canvas was clapped on. The boat bounded forward through a sea which seemed to be getting choppier. Luckily the wind was still behind them, but it would favour their pursuers too.

Poom!

The first far-off cannon-shot came rolling across the water. It was an ominous sound. The Austrians might not be yet within range of any of the fishing-boats, but, when they were, what chance of resistance would there be?

Hour by hour the boats scudded northwards like a flock of startled geese. Hour by hour the naval squadron closed the gap by almost imperceptible degrees. At least, thought Mark thankfully, it contained no steamers. It seemed to consist of a two-masted, square-rigged brig, mounting several guns, and three pinnaces. Not exactly an armada, but invincible against men armed only with rifles and pistols . . .

'It's impossible,' muttered Bilibin, 'it's only a matter of time. Why don't we run for the shore?'

'The men say that all this district is crawling with whitecoats,' Mark explained. 'The only chance is to make for the marshy stretch round Comacchio. It's so desolate there, we'd have some hope of hiding among the lagoons.'

The brig fired at intervals. One boat, dismasted, had already fallen behind and was being boarded by one of the pinnaces. Several others were taking in sail and making signs of surrender.

'It is the fishermen,' said Tessa, with tears of anger in her voice. 'They want to save their boats. And our men cannot manage by themselves.'

Aboard their own craft no one dared to speak of surrender. Throughout the rest of the night they ran before the wind, with the constant flash and rumble of gunfire astern. When day broke there were only half a dozen of the fishing-boats still in the race. All the others had been overhauled and their passengers made prisoner. Relentlessly the Austrian patrol-boats followed in the wake of the remainder.

'Comacchio,' said Ugo Bassi, pointing shorewards, and they saw the slender brick-red towers standing up from the low strip of land, bright in the first sunshine.

Garibaldi shouted an order to the helmsman. Slowly the figurehead swung round, the upraised trumpet pointed towards the desolate sand-dunes stretching green and gold beyond the little town. Glancing back, Mark saw that all but two of the flotilla had been taken. The pinnaces were still in hot pursuit and now the brig, afraid to come too close inshore for fear of sandbanks, had lowered her long-boat for the last mile of the chase.

Garibaldi measured the distance between boat and shore, between boat and pursuers. His blue eyes narrowed. Mark was near enough to see that it was true what people said — the man's eyes were remarkable, seeming to darken and change colour when he was moved. He raised his voice to carry the length of the crowded boat.

'Listen! We are going to beach the boat as near as we can get to those sand-dunes. The prisoners will be left — no one is to harm them. You will all scatter and save yourselves as best you can.' There was a murmur of disagreement from the redshirts. 'That is an order. It is every man for himself. No one is to wait for me, except Leggiero. No one.'

They all knew why Leggiero had been given his dangerous privilege. Not only was he one of Garibaldi's closest friends but he had been crippled in the siege of Rome and could not in any case move fast.

A protest rose to Tessa's lips, but Garibaldi stifled it. 'No one, child,' he repeated. 'I will take care of the Signora. Go with your friends. We must not bunch together in large parties.'

A few minutes later the boat grounded with a gentle shudder. It was the signal for all the volunteers to go over the side into the tawny shallows and wade ashore.

Far behind them came a sputter of rifle-shots but the range was too great. Mark and Bilibin seized Tessa, one each side, and rushed her through the water, over the yielding drifts of yellow sand, towards the shelter of the grass-tufted dunes. Mark's last glimpse of Garibaldi was of the General carrying Anita in his arms through the breakers, with Leggiero limping at his side. The other two boats had grounded further along the shore and were spilling their occupants.

It was extraordinary how quickly several dozen men could be swallowed up in that wilderness of hillock and shimmering grasses and brackish lagoons. Mark and his two friends followed a sandy track at random, running as fast as they could. They saw no more of the other fugitives, but suddenly they came face to face with a solitary young Italian. His face lit up at the sight of their red shirts.

'Where is Garibaldi?'

Tessa glared at him suspiciously. He was neither peasant, nor fisherman, nor soldier. He wore the dress of a middle-class townsman. What was he doing here, and at this hour of the morning?

He read the doubt in her face. 'You *must* trust me,' he said. 'My name is Bonnet — I am Garibaldi's friend — my younger brother was killed in Rome. I heard the guns during the night, I guessed it was Garibaldi. For the love of Heaven tell me where he is!' He turned and pointed back along the path. 'My servant is waiting on the road — I've a gig all ready——'

Tessa hesitated no longer. 'They're somewhere just behind us, *signore*. They're carrying the Signora, so they can't move fast. But hurry! The Austrians are very near.'

'I will find them, never fear. Hurry, yourselves, my friends. My gig won't hold any more.'

He ran on into the sand-dunes and disappeared.

They hurried on for another mile through a maze of sandy tracks winding between sheets of blue water and belts of whispering reeds. In the distance the red towers of Comacchio stood out as the sole signposts in an unknown region — but dared they go that way if the town was garrisoned by their enemies?

'We must,' said Bilibin, taking command.

'But, Mr. Bilibin——'

'We cannot stay here for ever. We must take a chance.' Even in that grim situation Mark could not repress a laugh: never had he expected to hear the cautious Bilibin use such a phrase. 'These reeds will shelter us,' said his tutor, slipping off the enormous knapsack which he had never abandoned throughout the long retreat. 'Tessa, you will have the goodness to turn your back while Mark and I get rid of these incriminating red garments. Unfortunately,' he continued in a muffled voice, as he struggled out of his shirt, 'although I brought something for this very emergency, so far as Mark and I myself are concerned, I did not have the forethought to provide any suitable item of feminine apparel.'

'Never mind, Mr. Bilibin. I can tie my big kerchief across my shoulders. That will hide most of my red shirt. How lucky that I was wearing a skirt when we left San Marino!'

When they faced each other again they saw a transformation. Bilibin and Mark were in white shirts, creased from long folding, but clean and respectable. Bilibin's two-day growth of beard was a pity, but it was less likely to be noticed here than in England. The glimpse of red under Tessa's kerchief would hardly arouse suspicion. The enemy would not be looking for young girls.

Sadly they rolled up the other two shirts and scraped the soft sand over them. Mark threw his rifle and cartridge-belt into the lagoon.

'We had better abandon our knapsacks, too,' said Bilibin. 'They look too military.'

'But — sir! We shall have only the clothes we stand up in.'

'We can buy anything we need, once we get safely to a town.' Bilibin tapped his waistline and they heard the reassuring clink of coins. 'I have a quantity of English sovereigns stitched into a canvas belt next to — er — my skin. With those we shall be all right anywhere.'

So the three of them trudged forward to the beckoning towers of Comacchio, empty-handed except for a small volume of Horace's *Odes*, which Bilibin declared he had had since Oxford and refused to part with now.

'And then, I suppose, your troubles were over?' said MacWhirter as the waiter brought them immense portions of suet pudding, welcome in the chilly autumn evening that was settling over London.

'Not quite over,' said Bilibin. 'We reached Comacchio without being challenged. We managed to install ourselves in an inn, we were able to equip ourselves with

necessaries and buy Tessa — er — a more suitable ward-
robe. But then the soldiers arrived and began searching
the whole town for strangers.'

'Mr. Bilibin was marvellous,' Mark interrupted with
enthusiasm. 'He didn't actually tell any untruths, but he
waved our papers at them, and Horace's *Odes*, and——'

'And an English sovereign,' said Bilibin dryly. 'It was
the Queen's head on that which seemed to convince
them of our nationality, far more than any document —
especially when I invited the sergeant to keep the coin
for reference.'

'And the lassie?'

'She talked English all the time they were there. They
were a little worried because she had no papers, but again,
as I said, they seemed quite ready to accept a coin instead.'

'Where is she now?'

'In Verona. We traced her relatives when we passed
through.'

'We wanted her to come back with us to England,'
said Mark, speaking perhaps more for himself than for
Bilibin. 'But she says Italy is her country and she's stopping there until the Austrians are kicked out.'

In the hotel coffee-room they talked of the other people
they had known in Italy. MacWhirter, now back in the
middle of the journalistic world, was able to give them
all the news they had missed during their slow journey
back across the Continent.

Anita Garibaldi was dead. She had died in Garibaldi's
arms, the day after their landing, in the lonely farmhouse
to which his friend had sent them for refuge. Garibaldi
and Leggiero had vanished, and, despite all the bribes

and threats of the enemy, no one knew where they were in Italy. MacWhirter had heard a rumour that they no longer *were* in Italy — that they had crossed the peninsula, taken ship from Tuscany, and were already on their way to America.

Ugo Bassi was dead, captured when hiding in Comacchio, and, though he had never broken his religious vows by taking arms, sentenced to death by firing squad.

Colonel Forbes, taken prisoner by the Austrian Navy, was now in a cell at Pola, but strong efforts were being made for his release and it was not likely that the Austrian Government would hold him much longer. Young Hugh Forbes had been hunted by the enemy when he left San Marino, but he had shown them a clean pair of heels. Mazzini was back in London.

It was growing late. The first October fog was rising from the Thames, seeping into the gaslit coffee-room. Italy seemed very far away. Then, clear above the noise of the cabs and carriages outside, they heard the twangling of a barrel-organ along the Strand.

'A bonny tune that,' said MacWhirter.

'Yes, sir. But I'd sooner hear *Fratelli d'Italia.*'

'Och, have ye not had enough of all that? You'll not be wanting to see Italy again for a while!'

'Perhaps not. But I keep remembering what Garibaldi said.'

'What was that, laddie?'

'He kept telling people, those last few days: "I shall be back in ten years." Perhaps *I* shall too.'

MacWhirter laughed and stretched his great limbs. 'Ten years, eh? I shouldn't wonder. Him — and you.

But meantime there's tomorrow. You and poor old Bilibin have got to face that terrifying old grandmother of
yours.'

'Yes, sir.' Mark smiled at his own thoughts and
memories. 'But somehow, you know, things are going
to be very different. Aren't they, Mr. Bilibin? We aren't
ever going to be afraid again.'

THE   END

PRINTED BY PURNELL AND SONS, LTD,
PAULTON (SOMERSET) AND LONDON

u/63